The Stoop

Steps leading to a lifetime of memories and
acceptance through music

G. Victor Moea

Fiction / Historical / Biographical / Music

The Stoop
Steps leading to a lifetime of memories and acceptance through music

by G. Victor Moea
www.TheStoopMusical.com

Cover design by: Elle Phillips
Edited by: Judy Thorburn
Victor's headshot by: Rictor Riolo
Content photos from: Camille & Bob Tartarilla

Personal Dynamics Publishing
www.PersonalDynamicsPublishing.com

ISBN: 978-0-9890889-4-7

Dedication

This book is dedicated to loving memory of my parents, Antoinette and George. Thank you for raising me in a neighborhood where I would discover a treasure chest of all beautiful people.

Preface

Growing up on the Lower East Side of Manhattan in the Williamsburg section of Brooklyn was a blast. My sister Marie and I discuss it quite often with so much joy. Although the family never had much in terms of finances, we look back and consider ourselves rich in more ways than one.

Every morning for 50 years my father would take a bus and two trains to get to work. He was a warehouseman laborer in New Jersey. My mother, for the most part, except for a short-term full-time job, was a stay-at-home mom. My father never owned a car, and everywhere we went we used public transportation or walked.

We were a very loving and close family who cared for one another very much. Our apartment was never considered just an apartment. It was always home, our home no matter where we had to live. We could never count the number of friends we had and all the activities we had at our fingertips living in a city with so many things to do. For example, there were activities such as stickball, punch ball, stoop ball, dances, singing doo-wop on street corners, just to mention a few and homemade activities created by street kids who had creative minds and great imaginations.

Growing up in an urban, very populated area allowed us the opportunity to get to know so many different types of people of all nationalities, religions, races, and many characters with different lifestyles. They were different in so many ways, all of which were very interesting, and this is one of the major factors that gave us the ability to become street smart.

Kids growing up in this type of environment experienced so much more of an education in learning about and understanding people, some of which can't be found in books. Formal educations are one thing, but without street smarts, how really educated are you? Street smarts are the education you acquire dealing with the real world and with real people. That is what growing up in this neighborhood environment teaches you.

There were a lot of poor people living on the Lower East Side. Some were extremely poor. My sister and I attended our Lady of Sorrows Catholic School. In my class were some very poor kids. We wore uniforms, and for the families who couldn't afford them, uniforms were given to them at no charge. Come Easter Sunday at mass, most of the kids wore new Easter outfits that their families could barely afford. They were never fancy or expensive, but nice. Meanwhile, the real poor kids wore their school uniforms for Easter mass, which for many, was the only dress clothes they had.

We were given free lunches. These lunches consisted of a peanut butter sandwich, or a jelly sandwich, or a cheese sandwich, or a butter sandwich, a soup of the day such as split pea, vegetable, tomato, or barley and milk and a dessert. Even to this day, these are still some of my favorite lunches.

After lunch was given out, whatever sandwiches were left over Sister Lucretia would gather up on a tray and go around to the classrooms asking if anyone wanted to take some home. Sister was always concerned that this lunch was, very possibly, the only full-meal some of the kids would eat that day.

Let me share with you a funny story about Sister Lucretia, the nun I had in third grade. She was a very short and petite lady in her 70s. I sat in the last seat of the first row of her classroom. Right behind my seat was the candy closet with a lock. I always loved to talk and socialize. To this day, I still do. On this particular day, sister was opening up the candy closet. I was talking and socializing and just having a good old time, when, POW, she hit me in the head with the lock and called me a curly top chatterbox.

You didn't dare go home and tell your parents that sister hit you in the head with a lock. My father would have hit me across my bottom with a stick and then asked "what did you do wrong?" Boy, how times have changed.

All of the nuns I ever had were great teachers and great disciplinarians. They were the extension to my home. They were our mothers during the day. I will never forget the love and the caring that they showed us and also the map they gave us to heaven. These ladies were certified and highly educated. They could have gone out in the world and made a good living. But instead, they chose to come to areas like the Lower East Side to teach kids like us. Their only pay was that of minimal donations. Yes, all of this and so much more are the beautiful memories growing up on the Lower East Side.

I love these United States of America and all the beautiful people in this country that struggle each and every day working hard, making a living and taking care of their families. Some of the wealthy weren't always wealthy and have never forgotten where they came from and are so willing to give back. There are also the senior citizens who have paid their dues wholeheartedly and who have contributed so much to this country; the Armed Forces who have fought and died for our country and are still doing so; the elderly couple who can barely take care of themselves tending to one another's needs; the children who bring so much joy to our country with their beautiful smiles and laughter; and the single-parent who is struggling sometimes with more than one job in fulfilling their responsibility with a loving obligation to their children.

This is my beloved country! I am thankful for the people, the opportunities, the freedoms, and so much more that are afforded to us, like no other country in the world. And to think, we wouldn't have this great place called America, if it wasn't for our immigrant ancestors who so bravely and willingly left their countries of birth to come to this beautiful new land and were willing to struggle so that their families and their descendants would be able to come to America; or those who were brought here against their will and struggled for their freedoms and their descendants to come here. We should all be so thankful to them and all the dreams they had for us, and never forget our loving immigrant ancestors ***and the beautiful gifts they left for us.***

~ Victor

Acknowledgements

To my six sons and all my daughters-in-law, who gave me magnificent and beautiful grandchildren, thank you for making so many of my dreams come true.

To my dearest friend Joe Sarlo, who encouraged me for many years to continue singing and was always there for me.

To my friends Camille and Jerry Duskin, who started Gateway Arts Foundation to help young people who are pursuing a career in the musical and performing arts. Thank you for making me a part of your foundation.

To all my family, friends, and acquaintances who have influenced me along my journey through life. You each had a part in making this book possible.

Thank you to Dr. Carole Altman, for all our heated debate sessions; and to her husband Milton, for refereeing all those discussions. We are just two New Yorkers going at it as usual.

To Ken Owens, who was a Godsend in guiding me in the publishing of this book.

To my beautiful wife Sigi, who is also my very best friend, and loves me 100%, but says she only likes me 99%. She is equally responsible for our book.

Much love to three ladies in heaven who had a great influence on this book; my sister Marie, my late wife Betty, and my mother-in-law Hilde.

Prologue

Welcome to my neighborhood. It's the 1950s on the Lower East Side of Manhattan, New York City, the most diversified area in the world. There were immigrants, first and second generations of every ethnicity, learning how to live together as one people, without prejudice of nationality, religion, race or choice of lifestyle. Everyone was struggling and working towards the common goal of a better life for themselves and their descendants.

Although the area was low income, it was very vibrant, rich in tradition loaded with energy and filled with adventurous, determined, rough-around-the-edges people. From this one geographic area emerged some of the most exciting and successful people in the world.

Every neighborhood has many stories. This story is about four kids, who came together to form a singing group, a doo-wop group as it was called at that time. Each one came from different ethnic backgrounds. They formed a relationship that would last a lifetime.

But before I start the story, let me give those of you who are not familiar with Manhattan's Lower East Side, a little profile on one of the first, if not the first, densely populated urban areas in the United States.

The horrible Irish potato famine created the first large influx of immigrants in the 1840s. During the turn-of-the-19th century, the United States welcomed the Ukrainians, Germans, Eastern Europeans, Polish, Czechoslovakians, Russians, Hungarians, the Italians and many from Mediterranean and Asian countries. Eastern European Jews made up the largest population of immigrants living on the Lower East Side, with Catholics as the second. The 1940s and 50s brought folks from Puerto Rico. Many immigrants coming into this country either stayed or passed through the Lower East Side on their way to other American destinations. Any new immigrant coming into this country took their share of prejudicial abuse and that is why pocket communities developed that enabled people to feel safe amongst their own because they understood one another's language, cultures and traditions.

The Irish and Italians couldn't stand one another. The Irish, who came to America first, laid claim to the turf, as did other nationalities that settled in different neighborhoods. But love conquers all, and in time, nationalities began to intermarry.

On Mulberry Street, Mott Street, Elizabeth Street, and other streets in Little Italy, apartment buildings were divided by what province of Italy you came from such as Naples, Bari, Sicily, etc. Back then, at the turn of the century, Sicilians weren't considered Italians.

Sicily is an island off the southern coast of the Italian peninsula. The only race and nationality that was brought to this country against their will was from the African continent. Unlike other immigrants coming into the country, their journey wasn't a dream for a better life. Their journey to America was an outrage. It was an atrocity, one of the worst treatments of human beings that ever took place in this country. And yet, their contributions to America were many. This book includes one of their contributions, which is a very large part of American music.

Starting in the 1930s, people lived together in either low-income public housing (projects), which were high-rise multi-dwellings, or the cold-water flats. Before some of these cold-water flats became multi-dwellings for immigrants coming into the country, they were single-family homes, which were converted into multi-dwellings. As more and more immigrants continued coming into our country, landowners saw the profit potential for building more tenements.

You may ask why they were called cold-water flats? They called them cold-water flats because you made your own hot water and heat. In each kitchen was a small water tank. Each water tank had a gas burner under it, which you lit with a match to heat the water. These tenements were usually brick, five-story, walk-up buildings, with many families on each floor. Some of the older tenements had a single bathroom in the hallway for all families on that floor to share. A bathtub in the kitchen also served as a washbasin to wash your laundry.

Before we had refrigerators, we had iceboxes to keep food cold. The icebox was made of wood and an iceman would deliver a block of ice to keep your food cold. There were fire escapes in the front or back of the building. These fire escapes were metal structures with steps going down to the ground floor in case of an emergency evacuation. The fire escape also served as a place for keeping your perishable foods cold in the winter months and a place to sleep on hot steamy nights, since there was no such thing as air-conditioning. A telephone pole in the backyard served as a connection for a clothesline. From this pole was a pulley that screwed into the side of your window frames. You would hang your laundry on the rope with clothespins and this, of course, is how you dried your laundry. Before electricity, there were gaslights for lighting the apartment and wood-burning or coal-burning potbelly stoves.

By the 1940s, change was taking place. There were gas stoves and refrigerators, although a few flats still had the tank in the kitchen for making their own hot water. Eventually, this all evolved into the modern conveniences we have today.

Some of the apartments were referred to as railroad rooms, which ran straight through the apartment like boxcars. One room was a kitchen, one room a living room, and the other two rooms, if you were lucky, were bedrooms. But if you had a lot of kids, forget the living room. You also had minimum amount of closet space.

Your garbage was put in paper bags and you would walk downstairs to the ground floor where there were metal garbage pails that the landlord of the building would put out on the street for twice a week trash pickup.

The rates were low and comparable to the times. Today, most of these apartments are high rentals or condominiums. If you are ever in New York's Lower East Side, I suggest you take a tour of the Old Tenement Museum located at 103 Orchard Street, in Lower Manhattan. Some of the tenement houses had steps, which led up to their entrance called stoops. The stoops had six, sometimes more, sometimes less, steps.

The stoop also served as a meeting place for tenants. After dinner, if the weather was nice, the tenants would sit outside with their chairs and socialize with one another. It was also a meeting place for young people to get together, socialize, and share schemes and dreams with one another, or just hang out. For some of the kids in the neighborhood, the stoop wasn't just an entrance to a building. It became their center of the universe. Some crowds would hang out on corners. Some crowds would hang out in luncheonettes. Some crowds would hang out in candy stores or ice cream parlors, but for the kids in this story, it was the stoop. The stoop was where it would all begin.

The streets were loaded with kids playing stickball, punch ball, stoop ball and any other game that they could invent. Every Sunday, if there weren't much going on, some of the guys would pitch pennies, nickels, dimes, and quarters. You would pitch up against a wall, and who ever came closest to the wall would win and pick up all the coins pitched. Then there was hit the coin. You would place a coin, usually a penny, on the ground. There would be two players, each one facing one another and each player five or six feet away from the coin. Using a rubber ball, each player would try to hit the coin. I'm telling you, there were so many games invented in the streets; simple games that cost nothing to play, and were just as exciting then, as any of today's computer games.

There were a variety of mom-and-pop stores such as delicatessens, grocery stores, candy stores, Chinese hand-laundries, bakeries, luncheonettes, and Latin bodegas, to mention a few. A multitude of synagogues and churches were also in the neighborhood, because, at that time, most of the Lower East Side was predominately Jewish and Catholic. Although there were a variety of ethnic groups living among one another, there were still divisions within the neighborhoods that had multi-ethnic groups living there.

People were skeptical of one another for the lack of understanding of traditions other than their own. Some of them were very close-minded, to say the least. In some homes, there were ethnic slurs used towards other nationalities and religions. But once the kids got out into the streets and started socializing and playing with one another, they recognized and felt something altogether different. Although not realizing it, they were giving one another a chance, and out of this came a fact. It wasn't what ethnicity or religion a person was, but instead, how good and respectful they were. It was the kids who opened the doors and showed a lot of adults how we all could get along, regardless of our ethnic background.

As mentioned earlier, there were pocket communities. Some of these neighborhoods would love to have your business, but frowned on anyone living in their neighborhood that wasn't of their ethnic group. Spanish Harlem, Black Harlem, Little Italy, Hell's Kitchen (Irish) and Chinatown were just a few that had their own neighborhood gangs. However, this wasn't the case on the Lower East Side along the East River where public housing was developed. These housing projects (as they were also referred to) started to be built in the 30s. Old and very distressed slumps were torn down to make rooms for public housing with modern upgrades that were never experienced before by so many poor and low-income families. They were built for poor and low-income families. Ethnic backgrounds weren't a factor. There was a wonderful blend of people of all nationalities, races and religions within the public housing projects at that time that respected one another and got along just fine.

A few kept to themselves, but eventually that changed. I don't know if the city planned it that way, or it just happened, but it worked. Other than in the projects, at times there were problems just walking through some of the pocket communities where everyone was just one race or one nationality. Some of the wise-asses in these communities would take it upon themselves to ridicule and disrespect those walking through their neighborhoods that were different from them.

A few of the public housing projects on the Lower East Side were Lillian Wald, Jacob Riis, Baruch Houses, Madison Street Houses, and Knickerbockers Village. At that time, the Jewish community made up 40% of the Lower East Side. In some of the Jewish owned stores, you couldn't help but notice the tattooed numbers on the arms of some of the owners and employees that were Holocaust survivors.

There were gang problems in the streets. There usually is in urban communities, but all in all, the majority of people living on the East Side were very hard-working family people, and the majority of kids were good kids and not gang members.

Singing and making music became a very popular pastime in the neighborhoods when the doo-wop craze hit in the 50s. This led some of the vocal groups to the professional level of entertainment. Doo-wop vocal groups were popping up in every neighborhood. Out of my neighborhood came four kids with different ethnic backgrounds. It was singing which brought them together, forming a lifetime bond of friendship and love for each other. This all takes place on what became their most sacred spot in their world, the stoop in the Lower East Side.

Come join me on *The Stoop*...

{ 1 }

It's a hot steamy summer day in 2019. Johnny (one of the vocal group members) is sitting on the stoop in the neighborhood where he grew up on the Lower East Side. Johnny is taken by how the neighborhood has changed. It's much cleaner and a lot more up-scaled.

A garbage truck is coming down the street collecting trash that's picked up in plastic bags, unlike the way it was back in the day when metal garbage pails were overflowing and the New York sanitation workers would be breaking their backs emptying those metal pails of garbage into the truck's hopper.

Johnny remembers the times when there was no alternate side of the street parking. Today, there are certain days you're not allowed to park on one side of the street and other days you're not allowed to park on the other side of the street. This was put into effect on those specific days so the garbage trucks had clear sailing to collect the trash, and sweepers would have clear sailing cleaning that side of the street which had no parked cars.

Johnny realizes even with the heat, there were no fire hydrants open. In his day, there would have been dozens of kids running in an out of the water that was spraying out of fire hydrants. The cops would come and close it. Once the cops left, ingenious kids would open it again with a hanger and a stick. Sure, we had a public pool, but nothing was more invigorating on a hot summer day or night than the cool waters of an open fire hydrant. Besides, Pitt Street Pool, which was the public pool on the Lower East Side, had long lines that sometimes wrapped around the corner. Some of the neighborhood adults even enjoyed stepping their feet into the cool water of the open fire hydrants. What a wonderful time it was.

The late 1960s and 1970s came along and with more change came the defacing of the Lower East Side. Drugs ran rampant. Crime escalated to the highest it had been since the late 1800s when Irish gangs fought one another as if it was the Wild West. A bad element began to infiltrate the Lower East Side. There were burnt-out buildings, graffiti and garbage everywhere. It looked like an *I don't give a damn* type of a neighborhood. But, with all of its devastation, it survived because of the many good hard-working people living there.

A Brooklyn kid by the name of Rudy Giuliani became the mayor of New York City. His love for the city, its good people, and his hate for crime changed things drastically, and the change was for the best. Johnny was so happy and proud to see the change that took place on his Lower East Side. Now you have posh restaurants. Cold-water flats and factories were refurbished to high-end magnificent condos and apartments. Today, The Lower East Side is predominantly Latino with a strong community and civic groups keeping the neighborhood beautiful and safe.

Johnny was in town to meet up with some of his friends that had shared so much together as kids. They were all going to meet on the stoop where in the past, it had become their monument, their pyramid, their stairway to the stars. After so many years, they were getting together once again to make plans and, of course, these plans had to be discussed on the stoop. You see, this is where it all began for four of these kids who did not know each other but came together to start a singing group, a doo-wop group, and a friendship that would last a lifetime. They were instrumental in bringing a neighborhood and its people closer with a better understanding of one another.

One of the guys came up with an idea to start a foundation, a scholarship fund which would help the kids of the Lower East Side who were interested in the musical arts. This would help so many talented kids who couldn't afford to take lessons. They called it the Lower East Side Gateway Arts Foundation, the gateway to a whole new exciting world. This was a great opportunity for kids who were interested in pursuing the performing arts. They believed that there was so much raw street talent and that all these kids really needed was a chance, a direction to cultivate their talent. They wanted to give these kids that chance.

{ 2 }

A big black limousine pulled up to the stoop and out steps *Georgie Mo*, otherwise known as George Joseph Molinski, one of the vocal group members. You see, in the neighborhood, nicknames were very common. Almost everybody had some kind of a nickname. Let me share with you some nicknames and how we got them. For starters, there was *Louie Short Arms*. Every time he had to come up with some money, his hands couldn't reach his pockets, as though he had short arms; talk about a cheapskate. Then there was *Frankie Eye*. He lost one of his eyes as a kid in a rock fight, so he was tagged Frankie eye. How cruel!

Next, was *Stella the Stilt*. She stood 5'11" with legs that went to her neck. At that time, she was bigger than any kid in the neighborhood. Let me tell you about one more, for now, who was called *Beansie*. Beansie thought he was a tough guy and acted like he knew it all. He had a brain the size of a bean with no common sense, or street smarts, and a mouth that was constantly getting him into trouble.

Sometimes names were given to people who were the exact opposite of how they really were. When we refer to someone as not having balls, it had nothing to do with male genitals. Having balls was our way of saying an individual was tough, not afraid, and had no fears. *Frankie Balls* was the exact opposite. He was afraid of everything and I mean everything, a complete nervous wreck. As we go on with the story you'll hear more nicknames.

Georgie Mo's mother and father were Polish immigrants. They owned one of the best Polish delis on the East Side known for their Polish sausage.

Georgie Mo stepped out of the limo and embraced Johnny. "Johnny Gun you old broken down antique, good to see you."

They called him *Johnny Gun* because he had tremendous arms. His real name was Giovanni Patrick Shea. Yeah, you guessed it. He was second generation Irish and Italian. His mother was first generation Italian. His father was first generation Irish. For the times, it was considered a mix marriage. The Irish and Italians hated one another, but love conquers all, and hate goes right down the drain where it belongs.

Johnny and Georgie grew up together. They attended the same Catholic grammar school, Our Lady of Sorrows, then Seward Park High School. The two boys were never the brightest kids in the class because their minds were set on less schoolwork and more socializing. If socialization was a subject, the two would have been "A" students.

In high school a new world opened up to them. They had more freedom to move around the school, going from class to class. That bit of freedom gave them the opportunity to harmonize in the school corridors, in the bathrooms and really anywhere they could get an echo. They both had good voices, but they didn't know much about harmony. That would come later.

This was the beginning of the doo-wop craze and local neighborhood vocal groups were springing-up all over the place, mimicking the groups of the day such as Frankie Lymon and the Teenagers, the Cleft Tones, the Schoolboys, the Harptones, and many more.

And then, of course, for Johnny and Georgie, there were the girls. They were both good-looking guys. The girls would swoon over Johnny, but he would never let it go to his head. He wasn't that type of a guy. Georgie, on the other hand, loved the attention and would play the role to the fullest. Johnny was a tough kid. Nobody would mess with him, but he wasn't a bully. In fact, Johnny was always for the underdog and was liked by everyone. He had a very compassionate and caring soul and was very sociable.

Johnny grew up in a household of singers. His mother, Antoinette, as a young girl, was an Italian singer and appeared on stage at the famous Brooklyn Academy of Music and on many Italian radio stations. In her day, a young woman from an Italian family would rarely be allowed to go on the road to promote herself or entertain around the country. Eventually, a young woman's career would come to a halt in order to prepare for marriage and raising a family the Old Italian way.

Johnny's father, Patty, was an Irish cop with a great Irish tenor voice. He loved singing World War I patriotic songs and, of course, the Irish tunes. He sang them with much vigor. He would get up and sing anywhere he had the opportunity and the people listening to him loved every minute. At any bash or racket, (as a party or dance was referred to), or any holiday when people got together, friends, relatives, sometimes whole neighborhoods, everybody would sing. It made no difference if you didn't know how to sing. Everyone just enjoyed themselves and sang along! Johnny's family always encouraged him to sing. He thought about becoming a cop for a while, but the love for music and singing was in his heart.

Georgie Mo was very much into himself. He was a tease and the biggest ball breaker in the neighborhood, especially when it came to the girls. He would tease, tease, and tease. Georgie's father wanted him to come into the family business, but Georgie wouldn't think of it at that time. All he wanted to do was sing, tease, and be a clown. Georgie would stop at every other store window to catch his reflection while he combed his hair. He can't do that anymore since he lost his hair, but he now sports a very expensive toupee.

Coming up the street was 6'4" tall Lawrence (*Big Larry B*) Bentley the III, a very spirited and very humorous African American Gent. Larry is credited with giving the vocal group their sound. Also coming on the block, just about the same time, was Paul (*Paulie Red*) Fleishman. Paulie Red is a sophisticated, very intelligent, soft spoken and very down to earth fellow of Hungarian Jewish descent. They all begin to embrace one another with hearts full of joy. They're together once again sharing their longtime friendship, love and respect for one another, which brought them back to the neighborhood after so many years. Reminiscing, they plan to give back to their neighborhood some of the wonderful things that the neighborhood has given them. To think, it all began on a stoop for four kids. Four kids (Johnny, Georgie, Larry and Paulie), each with different ethnic backgrounds, but sharing their common love for singing and making music with their voices. Music is free of prejudice. It brings all people together. It's magical!

{ 3 }

Larry recalls the first time he met Georgie and Johnny, and the guys began to reminisce about the old days. Johnny and Georgie were sitting on the stoop trying to harmonize and never getting it right. Larry was very enterprising. Across the street from the stoop was Izzy's barber shop where Larry had the shoeshine concession in front of the barber shop. He made a deal with Izzy some months prior to build a shoeshine stand and pay Izzy a monthly fee for the space. Izzy liked the idea and Larry was in business. Larry built a state-of-the-art movable shoeshine station that he was able to move inside when the weather got bad.

Against his mother's wishes, Larry quit school with only a year left, to help his mother because he lost his father in World War II. His mother worked evenings cleaning offices. This never sat well with Larry. He made a promise that someday he would give his mother everything. Believe me, he stuck to that promise in a way that you would never imagine. Larry and his mother lived in the projects, the very same projects where Johnny and his family lived.

Mrs. Bentley was a wonderful woman. When the group finally got together she would allow them to use her apartment in the evenings for rehearsal so the guys wouldn't annoy the neighbors sitting out on the stoop. For days on end, Georgie and Johnny would be on the stoop trying to harmonize with no avail. Larry had to listen to these unusual vile sounds which were getting on his nerves. One day Larry approached Johnnie and Georgie to tell them off…"If that's harmony you're trying to do, you're not even close. You sound like two cats in heat. You're annoying and you're disturbing to my customers, as well as to a lot of other people in the neighborhood." Larry was a very funny comedic guy, very spirited with a great sense of humor.

Georgie took offense, "So what are you? A professor of harmony?"

Larry replied, "I'm not a professor but, I know enough about harmony to know that you don't."

Johnny responded in his low key gentlemanly fashion, "Maybe you can give us a few pointers. Anything would be appreciated."

Georgie chimed in, "If you're so great, show us something so we're not so annoying to you and your customers and everyone else on the block."

Larry began to walk away, stopped, turned around, and said, "Maybe I will, so I won't have to listen to these annoying sounds and be able to concentrate on my work in peace."

"What's your name?" Johnny asked.

Larry replied, "Lawrence Bentley III. If, and when I get to know you, and if, and when I get to like you, then, and only then, you can call me Larry, but not until then. You got it?"

Larry asked, "What's your name?"

Johnny replied, "Seeing how we're getting so formal, the name is Giovanni Fitzpatrick Shea. You can call me Johnny Gun whenever you choose to. This gentleman to my right is George Joseph Molinsky, but you can call him Georgie Mo."

Larry began to show them the proper way to use their voices when doing harmony. It didn't take long. Georgie and Johnny couldn't believe their sound, especially when Larry added his note getting a full three-part harmonic sound.

"That was good. You got the idea. You two guys did two-part harmony and I added the third part. Well, whatcha think?"

Johnny and Georgie looked at one another in amazement. They finally learned how to do harmony, and with Larry filling in the third voice, their dream of starting a vocal doo-wop group was on the horizon.

Larry then said, "Goodbye. Now I can get back to my business and hear some good sounds coming from you guys. It's going to be a little more pleasing to the ear."

Georgie and Johnny would practice for hours every day and would enjoy every minute of it. Johnny discussed with Georgie the possibility of Larry joining the group. Georgie was a little hesitant about having to sing with a black guy. Johnny never even gave it a thought. He was that type of a guy. Johnny and Georgie sat on the stoop discussing Larry.

"Who cares what a person is," Johnny told Georgie. "It's how people are that really matters, and that guy Larry seems like a real decent guy and besides, did you ever hear a voice better than that?"

Georgie began to agree with Johnny but added, "He never better act like a big shot just because he taught us harmony, or I'll kick his ass!"

Johnny humored Georgie, "Yah, yah, yah. Spoken like a real tough guy."

{ 4 }

A few weeks passed and Johnny approached Larry, "Hi Larry, how's business?"

Larry had some suspicions. "The neighborhood is nice and peaceful since you guys learned a little harmony. How's it coming along Johnny?"

"Well, we practiced a lot and we remembered everything you taught us. But, I have a question," Larry curiously responded, "Question, what's the question?"

Johnny stumbled with his words a bit. "Look Larry, I'm not going to beat around the bush. Would you be interested in joining a group that we're forming? Before you answer, let me explain what's happening here. There's a city-wide competition for vocal doo-wop groups and the winner gets a recording contract. Win or lose, just to participate would be great. Would you be interested?"

Larry, in his spirited and comedic way looked up at Johnny, "Are you crazy man? What would my fans think if I were to sing with a bunch of Caucasian fellows? This could ruin my reputation!"

Georgie Mo began to break Larry's balls. "Just think of it Larry. We can make history by being one of the first multi-racial doo-wop groups, and it can all happen because you chose to sing with us. You can become one of the most famous people in the world, even more famous then Mickey Mouse, himself. Look what you could be giving up if you don't sing with us."

Johnny continued, "I'm not asking you to marry my sister. Besides, the world is changing. What does singing have to do with what you are?" It's like I told Georgie Mo, "It's not what you are. It's how you are, and I happen to like who you are. You're a little nutty, but a good guy."

Larry and Johnny walked over to the stoop. Larry informed Johnny, "You know Johnny, I already heard about this competition. The groups will come from all over to compete and try to make a name for themselves. The groups are not only from New York, but also from New Jersey, Pennsylvania, Connecticut, and who knows where else. It's going to take a lot of work and a lot of sacrifice and a whole lot of energy. If I decide to come on board, there is a condition, and here it is. I am the vocal director of the group, and I'll have no complaining. Do we understand one another? I sure hope so, because my time is very valuable. I don't want to hear halfway down the road that this is too much for you guys!"

Johnny put his hand out and shook hands with Larry and said, "Your conditions are met. I give you my word and thanks a lot Larry."

Larry reminded Johnny that they needed a fourth singer in the group, a good lead singer with an excellent voice.

{ 5 }

The crowd hanging out on the stoop consisted of a couple of dozen guys and girls. It sure resembled the United Nations. Some were out of high school and working, and some were going to college. Of course their where always the guys who wanted nothing to do with school. God bless the Jews. They were always big on education.

Johnny and Georgie were out of school and had jobs. Georgie worked for his father in the deli and hated every minute of it. Georgie's father told him that now that he was out of school and had no intensions of attending college, he was not going to support him anymore. He had to work for his money.

Johnny worked on Wall Street as a runner for the Stock Exchange biding his time waiting for his opportunity to make his living in the music and recording industry. Johnny also played a little guitar, enough to back himself when he sang solo.

Johnny was 18 years old. In the 1950s, you were allowed to go into bars and drink at age 18. Even though Johnny wasn't a drinker, in the evenings and on the weekends, Johnny would go into some of the local bars and sing for the patrons. He never got paid. He was never looking to get paid. All he wanted to do was to sing, and now that the group was forming, this was an opportunity to make his mark in the music industry.

In the evenings after work, everyone would meet by the stoop. If it was raining or too cold, they would hang out in one of the project hallways until a security guard came and kicked them out. In that case they would go to one of the ice cream parlors. But the stoop was the center of their universe, their secure hub where they were in control of everything that went on in the neighborhood. This is where it was happening.

This was their world. The stoop also served as the place where these kids would get together to share their ideas with one another and their life's dreams, what they wanted to do, and how they wanted to do it in their future lives; where boy meets girl and the wonders of love and romance began. Some of the elderly women would sit by their window and look out over the neighborhood, wanting to know what was going on, wanting to know everyone's business.

Mrs. Horowitz, one of the tenants in the building, would yell at the kids hanging out on the stoop when things got a little too loud. With her very heavy Yiddish accent she would yell, "Get off the stoop. Go make noise somewhere else. Go on your own stoops! Vatta you vant here?"

Georgie Mo would yell up to her, mimicking her Yiddish accent with something like, "I vant a piece ah bread and butter, ah cookie, maybe."

In response, Mrs. Horowitz would call Georgie Mo a mishugana (in Yiddish it means crazy) or a bum. Those were her pet names for Georgie Mo. He would tell her, "Someday, Mrs. Horowitz, I'm gonna kiss you and make crazy passionate love to you."

She would respond, "Never in a million years you bum! I'm a vidow. I don't do them things. I'm a good girl."

As I mentioned before, the crowd on the stoop consists of all kinds of characters, personalities, nationalities, races, religions and lifestyles. We all found a way of having a lot of fun, and we were always there for one another.

{ 6 }

Up the block from the stoop was a synagogue. Because there was no air-conditioning during the summer months, the synagogue doors and windows would be wide open. If you were passing by, you would hear the beautiful, majestic voice of the Cantor rehearsing and performing the service.

Enrico Caruso, a world renowned opera star of the early 1900s, used to study the voice techniques of some of the great Jewish cantors.

One in particular, was the world renowned, Cantor Yusuf Rosenblatt. Yusuf Rosenblatt was in one of the first talkie movies, the Jazz Singer, starring Al Jolson.

Every day a young Jewish kid about the age of 17 would pass by the stoop. He looked like a real nerd and walked like one, too. He wore big framed black horn rimmed glasses, had fiery red hair, dressed very plain, wore a yarmulke, and carried loads of books. Georgie Mo, of course, couldn't let it go. He had to tease him, saying things like, "Do windshield wipers come with them glasses?"

This particular day Georgie, Larry and Johnny were on the stoop. They heard this beautiful angelic voice coming from somewhere. It couldn't have come from a radio, because there was no music. It was just a beautiful voice. They followed the sound that led them to the synagogue. Georgie and Larry waited out by the curb while Johnny walked up the steps of the synagogue, opened the door and looked in. Johnny closed the door and turned around to face the guys with a look of amazement.

Larry questioned Johnny, "Why the face Johnny? You look like you just saw a ghost!"

Johnny answered, "You're not gonna believe who that voice belongs to!"

At that moment the door to the synagogue opened and out walked the nerd that passed the stoop every day. When he saw Johnny and the guys standing there he thought he was going to get teased and harassed, so he started to back up.

Johnny approached him. "Where did you learn how to sing like that?"

The young fellow answered, "My father is the Cantor of this synagogue and I would like to follow in his footsteps."

Johnny questioned him, "Are you only allowed to sing Holy songs?"

The young man replied, "My father told me that all songs are Holy songs as long as you sing them from your heart."

Johnny asked him his name, to which he replied, "My name is Paul Fleischman."

Paul asked, "Why do you tease me, because I'm a Jew, and I don't dress and look like you guys?"

Referring to Georgie, Johnny said, "Do you see that tall ugly guy standing over there; the guy combing his hair? Well, he's got nothing better to do but make a complete asshole out of himself sometimes, but he really is a good guy. He's just a big pain in the ass. And no, that's not the case. We have a lot of Jewish friends. We got all kinds of friends. Besides, it's not what a person is, but how they are."

Johnny wanted to ask Paul to join the group but he didn't know the right way to approach him. He didn't want to offend him. He saw Paul as a very religious guy who might be all about religion and religion only. Paul was a little more liberal than the average religious Jew, especially when it came to music. He liked it all. Actually, he was a little more liberal than his family wished him to be, but he was very respectful to his family and to their religion.

Johnny started beating around the bush and was very surprised by Paul's response. He asked Paul if he knew anything about doo-wop music and the groups of the day. Paul answered by naming some of the groups of the day, "You mean Frankie Lymon and the Teenagers, the

Cleft Tones, the Dells? I like these groups, and I like what they do."

Johnny asked, "You mean you would sing this music if you had the chance to?"

With a cautious look still on his face, Paul stated, "I hear you guys practicing and you're pretty good. I never would imagine that you would ask a person like me to join your group. You are asking me to join your group?"

With a surprised look, Johnny said, "Yeah, we would like that very much."

Paul answered, "I'll give it a try!"

Johnny turned to Larry and Georgie Mo with the sound of relief and joy in his voice, "Well, here is our fourth voice; our lead singer that we've been looking for. From now on your nickname is *Paulie Red*."

{ 7 }

Johnny turned to Larry, "Larry, so now what?"

In a stern tone of voice, Larry proceeded in stating his case, "Now the work begins, the intense practicing, four, five nights a week, sacrificing, no more hanging out for a while, no more joking around, complete concentration to fulfill a dream which we all share, a love for singing, to be the best vocal group we could be. Nothing's gonna stop us now."

The guys were sticking to their end of the deal that they made with Larry at the inception of the group, when Larry said there would be a lot of hard work and no complaining. They finally found a way to keep Georgie from being a pain in the ass, and to keep him singing. Mrs. Bentley, Larry's wonderful mother, would allow them to use her apartment to practice while she was out working in the evening. She was a beautiful human being.

One evening, Mrs. Bentley arrived home early so the guys thanked her and were about to leave, but Mrs. Bentley wouldn't have it. She graciously asked the boys if they would stay and sing for her. You see, no one, up until this point, had ever heard them sing as a vocal group, not their parents nor any of the crowd. Mrs. Bentley became their first fan. Mrs. Bentley loved what she heard and asked the fellows if they had a name for the group.

Larry, "You know, we were so intense with our singing, a name for the group never came to mind. We need a name!"

Paulie Red suggested, "Because Larry is always telling us to keep the harmony tight and to keep it mellow, how about Harmony?"

They thought about it for a while then Johnny said, "I like it, I really like it."

Larry agreed, but Georgie was being his same old shithead self. "Oh, I don't know. It's nice, but I don't know."

Larry looked at Georgie, "Come on you gas pain! Stop breaking our chops!"

Georgie smiled back, "I like it. I really do like it."

Later that same evening while the group was practicing, they heard a lot of ambulance activity in the neighborhood.

The following day, when Georgie and a local neighborhood girl named Frannie walked over to the stoop, they were told that Mrs. Horowitz had a heart attack the night before and was taken to the hospital. Out of character, Georgie panicked and wanted to know what hospital they took her to. Georgie grabbed

Frannie's hand and they ran as fast as they could to the hospital.

In the lobby of the hospital there was a flower shop. Georgie bought flowers to bring to Mrs. Horowitz. Frannie was surprised. She had never seen Georgie act like this before. When they entered Mrs. Horowitz's room, her eyes were closed.

Georgie stood over her bed and in a whisper called her name, "Mrs. Horowitz, Mrs. Horowitz, it's me Georgie. I came to visit you."

Mrs. Horowitz opened her eyes and said, "I get a heart attack and the first person I see when I open my eyes is the bum, the mishugana (crazy-nuts) and he brings me flowers, too!"

Georgie told Mrs. Horowitz that he will never tease her again and pleaded for her to forgive him? Georgie asked Mrs. Horowitz, "Mrs. Horowitz, may I kiss you goodbye?"

Mrs. Horowitz replied, "A kiss maybe, but forget the mad passionate love. I'm not that kind of girl. I'm a good girl!"

{ 8 }

Sometimes there were new faces that joined the crowd. They came from other neighborhoods and sometimes from as far as

Brooklyn, which, to a lot of kids on the Lower East Side, was another world. This one time, Frannie, a gum chewing feisty Irish girl, who

always had a wad of gum in her mouth and was part of the neighborhood crowd, informed the guys that a bunch of girls who she worked with in a typing pool were coming to visit her. The bunch of girls wanted to meet the rest of the crowd. Frannie sternly reminded all of them to behave themselves. The guys assured Frannie that they would be complete gentleman. But, of course, that wasn't the case at all.

The girls came from an area in Brooklyn called Ocean Parkway. This was considered a very uppity area. When the girls showed up on the block, the guys just dug in and did nothing but tease them all night. Georgie Mo, of course, was the leader of the pack. Despite the teasing, the girls endured. They thought the guys were a lot of fun. They never met characters like them before.

One of the girls from Brooklyn, Flora, had an instant crush on one of the guys that blossomed into something big, as time went on. We'll discuss that later.

Frannie was a complete lady all night until the girls left. You see, Frannie and Georgie were always at one another's throats. Frannie, having seven brothers, wasn't afraid of any guy. She started punching Georgie in the arms and in the chest, but Georgie just laughed it off, as he always did.

Georgie stated, in a demanding tone, "Hey Frannie, run and get me an Italian ice."

Frannie answered, "Are you crazy? That's four blocks away."

Georgie, with his goofball humor replied, "So walk. I'll wait."

One of Georgie's forte's was to be the neighborhood ball breaker, especially when it came to Frannie.

Isn't it strange how people can be close to you, even on a daily basis, and you never notice them?

They can pass you every day, almost rub shoulders with you, and yet we don't see them? This was the case with Johnny and a young Latino girl named Carmen.

Carmen lived in the tenement where the kids hung out on the stoop. She lived there with her mother Manuela and her father Louis and a few brothers and sisters. Carmen's mother and father came from Puerto Rico, but Carmen was born in New York. They lived in Spanish Harlem before coming to the Lower East Side. Carmen's mother was a homemaker, as it was for so many women back in the day. As a young woman, Carmen's mother pursued a singing career, but gave it all up when she met her husband, Louis. Carmen's father was a factory worker who worked very hard, as so many men did to provide for their families.

There were many unskilled workers who came to this country. Whatever job they were given, they learned it well, and became skilled in what they did. To build a city like New York, they were more than just a common laborer, as they were referred to by many. They were geniuses who turned ordinary laboring into a fine meticulous craft, which is very difficult finding today.

Carmen worked in a bathing suit factory. She would arrive home every evening about five thirty, run-up the stoop unnoticed by any of the crowd sitting on the stoop and entered the tenement.

This went on for some time. She was quiet, very plain looking, even a little tattered looking, very shy, and kept to herself. She would notice Johnny. In time, she developed quite a crush on him, but Johnny showed no interest. Johnny would, every once in a while, give Carmen a passing glance and a quick hello.

During her lunch hour, when the weather was nice, Carmen and a few of her girlfriends would sit outside in front of the factory and sing. Carmen was a natural and had a beautiful singing voice, and like her mother, had aspirations of someday becoming a singer, but knew as long as she was living in her father's home, this would never happen. Singing was something forbidden by her father.

One day as she was sitting in front of the factory singing, a gentleman stopped, as so many passersby did, to listen. Being impressed with her voice, he gave Carmen his business card and asked if she would like to audition in his Greenwich Village nightclub. Carmen was thrilled and couldn't wait to get home to tell her mother. Arriving home she was busting at the seams with excitement. Hugging her mother, she told her she had wonderful news about an audition. Carman was very concerned with how her father would react, since he believed that a woman should be a wife and a mother and her place was at home.

Manuela responded to Carmen by telling her, "Mi hija (my daughter), go out in the world and pursue your dream as long as you never hurt yourself or anyone else." That was Friday and Carmen's audition was set for the following Saturday.

Carmen was excited because the week seemed to pass quickly. Saturday was here, the day of her big audition. Before she left the apartment that evening for her audition, Carmen spent some quiet time with her mother. She sat by her mother on the sofa, cuddled up in her mother's arms, as her mother would sing her a beautiful song. The words to the song went like this:

AS A LITTLE CHILD I DREAMED OF YOU
AND KNEW ONE DAY I'D BE SEEING YOU
NOW WE'RE TOGETHER AND I'M HOLDING YOU
MI HIJA (MY DAUGHTER) I LOVE YOU

AS A CHILD YOU WOULD LOOK UP TO ME
LIKE A GUIDING LIGHT FOR YOU TO SEE
THEN YOU WOULD REACH AND TAKE MY HAND GENTLY
MI HIJA, I LOVE YOU

AT TIMES IT WAS HARD WATCHING YOU GROW
TO KNOW ONE DAY I MUST LET YOU GO
WITH ALL OF MY HEART AND SOUL I WOULD PRAY
SO WHEN THAT DAY CAME YOU WOULD KNOW YOUR
WAY

YOU'RE NOT THAT BABY SITTING ON MY KNEE
MY PRAYERS WERE ANSWERED AND NOW YOU MUST
BE
THE WOMAN GOD MADE FOR THE WORLD TO SEE
MI HIJA, I LOVE YOU

YO TE AMO, MY DAUGHTER MI HIJA
I LOVE YOU, LOVE YOU, I DO!

{ **9** }

Saturday evening came. Paulie was home with his family, celebrating the end of the Sabbath. Georgie, Larry, and Johnny were just mellowing out on the stoop discussing some of their plans. Except for the light over the entrance to the tenement at the top of the stoop, all the shades to the apartments were drawn with no light coming through, except for one window.

Johnny was standing out on the curb of the sidewalk leaning up against a street lamp facing the tenement when something caught his eye coming from the only window with the shade drawn and the light coming through. It seemed to be the image of a woman getting dressed, but Johnny couldn't be sure. He wanted to see more, but the light went out. Georgie and Larry were sitting on the stoop with their backs to the entrance of the tenement. Johnny was facing the two guys and the entrance to the tenement when the door to the tenement opened. There was just enough overhead light to show a magnificent image of a woman standing at the top of the stoop. It was Carmen. The stoop never looked so good. Johnny looked up staring. He couldn't remove his eyes as Carmen made her way down the stoop, slowly, step by step by step, with all the elegance and the charm of a most sophisticated lady. Georgie and Larry stood up to let her pass as though she was royalty without a word being spoken. That was unusual for Georgie Mo. Johnny's eyes followed Carmen as she walked away leaving Johnny wondering. Who was she? Where is she from? Is she visiting someone in the tenement? Questions were running through Johnny's mind like wildfire. He had to know more about her, so Johnny decided to follow Carmen. He followed her from a distance to the Greenwich Village nightclub thinking that she was going to meet someone, never imagining that she was about to sing at the club. Johnny sat at the bar, looking around for Carmen, but did not see her anywhere in the crowd.

A little time passes, and the master of ceremonies came to the stage announcing, "Good evening ladies and gentlemen. Tonight we have a special guest, with a voice of a nightingale. I give you Lady Latina!" It was a name the owner felt was most fitting for this beautiful lady, Carmen, who began to sing.

Johnny was thinking about this beautiful woman with such a beautiful voice and wondering where she came from, who she was, and why he was falling in love. Johnny kept on staring at Carmen while she was on stage, and kept asking himself if he'd ever seen her before. She looked a little familiar to Johnny, but did he ever meet her before? He did not realize that he did meet her, but not in that light. Carmen finished her show at the club with great success. It was wonderful. The audience, as well as the boss, enjoyed every minute of it. The boss offered Carmen a job singing at the club on weekends and joyfully, she accepted.

Carmen noticed Johnny in the crowd sitting at the bar, but didn't let on. Her heart was pounding like a drum, but she played it very cool and nonchalant. Carmen said good night to everyone and left the nightclub for home aware that Johnny was following her from a distance. She began to wonder what Johnny's next move was going to be. Of course, he followed her right to the tenement. As she started making her way up the steps to the stoop, she turned and asked Johnny, "Excuse me, but are you following me?"

Johnny replied, "Do I know you? Do you live in this building? I've never seen you before, but somehow I know you from somewhere."

Carmen answered, "Yes I live in this building. I've been living here for the past three years."

Johnny was confused. "How come I've never noticed you before?"

Carmen was still acting cool and nonchalant, as her heart was beating double time as she questioned Johnny. "What is it you want? Can I help you?"

In a soft voice, Johnny says, "I just want to meet you. My name is Johnny. What's yours?"

"My name is Carmen. I pass you every night coming home from work going up to my apartment."

Johnny hesitated for a while in deep thought. He was thinking, who can she be?

Carmen then asked Johnny, "Please wait one minute. I'll be right back." Carmen ran up to her apartment, put on that funny little hat she wore to work every day, and came back out on the stoop.

Johnny, "You're that little girl with that funny little hat pulled down almost covering your eyes that flies up the steps every night after work, aren't you?"

Carmen replied, "Maybe. So what if I am? Why do you want to meet me?"

Johnny very softly answered, "Because, I never really met you before, and I would like to meet you now for the first time. You're beautiful."

Carmen's heart was still beating like a bongo drum. "Let me begin by introducing myself. My name is Giovanni Fitzpatrick Shea. They call me Johnny Gun. And yours?"

"My name is Carmen Maria Consuela Quinones", she replied.

Johnny, in turn stated, "It's so nice to meet you, Carmen Maria Consuela Quinones."

Carmen responded back, "It's finally so nice to meet you, Giovanni Fitzpatrick Shea, Johnny Gun." She said this with a smile on her face that just about lit up the neighborhood. With both hearts pounding, they sat on the stoop and talked to the wee hours of the morning. A romance began; one that would last a lifetime. Where did it all begin? But of course, on the stoop!

{ **10** }

Johnny and his family were about to move out of the neighborhood to the Williamsburg section of Brooklyn, a neighborhood similar to the Lower East Side. This section of Brooklyn was right across the Williamsburg Bridge. Crossing over the East River it was a short bus ride from the Lower East Side where Johnny and his family would be residing.

Back in 1949, a movie was made called "City Across the River." The river was the East River, and the city wasn't a city, but a section of Brooklyn called Williamsburg. The reason

Johnny's family had to leave the projects was because his mother took a part-time job and failed to notify the project management. This put Johnny's family in a little higher pay scale and your rent was based on the family income. Someone told the office management that Johnny's mother had a part-time job that was never reported, so the office management wanted all the back rent that was owed to them. Johnny's family couldn't afford the back rent, and they were asked to leave.

Johnny and his sister Marie were born in a cold water tenement in Brooklyn and now they were moving back to a cold water tenement in Brooklyn. This wasn't going to keep Johnny from hanging out on the Lower East Side. He had his vocal group there, and he had Carmen.

Every night after work, Johnny would go down to the Lower East Side and practice with the group where they would put in 4 to 5 hours each night rehearsing. Sometimes Johnny would stay over at one of the guy's apartments. Up until that time no one had heard the group sing except for Mrs. Bentley.

Paulie suggested that the group sing at a dance that was taking place at one of the settlement houses on the Lower East Side. The dance would be on a Saturday night, and the whole neighborhood would be there. This might be the perfect time to show their wares and get good feedback from the crowd.

It was all set. The group would debut at the Lower East Side Settlement House. The Lower East Side had a lot of settlement houses. These establishments came into existence at the turn of the century when immigrants were coming into the Lower East Side. The settlement houses would find living quarters for the immigrants as well as jobs. In time, the settlement houses became recreational centers with a lot of after-school activities as well as summer programs for the neighborhood kids. They still exist to this day.

Paulie still hadn't told his father about the singing group and his newfound friends. He told his mother and promised her that he would tell his father when the time was right, or rather, until he built up enough courage.

Paulie's father came to the United States from Hungry in the 1920s. He was a very educated man, had a beautiful voice, and eventually became a Cantor, following in his father's footsteps.

This particular evening Paulie approached his father and asked if he could speak with him. "Papa, I met a bunch of fellows, three of them, that wanted to start a singing group and they asked me to sing with them. At first Papa, I was very hesitant why I wanted anything at all to do with these fellows, but they proved to be a great bunch of guys who are very respectful. They like me, Papa, and like us, love

69

to sing. It's not the kind of songs that you would do, but you told me that any song is a holy song as long as you sing from your heart. You see Papa, a contest is going to take place with vocal groups from all over the city and beyond competing for a chance to win a recording contract. Papa, if you're wondering if I'm having any change of heart of following in your footsteps and becoming a Cantor, Papa you need never to worry. To be a Cantor is my dream, Papa, as well as your dream for me."

Mr. Fleischman hesitated for a short while then asked, "Paul, what do you call this kind of music?"

Paul explained to his father, "It's called doo-wop, Papa, doo-wop

Mr. Fleischman: "Doo-wop. It's a funny name for a style of singing, but then again the word jazz was probably also considered a funny word, and for your information, my son, I also enjoy a little jazz myself."

Paulie: "Does that mean, Papa, that I have your blessing?"

Mr. Fleischman: "And when do I get to meet and hear your group? I would like for you to invite them over to our home tomorrow evening to sing for me and Mama."

Paulie kissed and hugged his father, thanking him, and assuring him that tomorrow evening would be fine. The next evening the boys arrived at Mr. and Mrs. Fleischman's home and were greeted so cordially and made to feel so welcomed. Mrs. Fleischman put milk and cookies on the table. The guys thought that was great, a mother who always sees her son and his friends as little boys. After some chatter at the dining room table the boys began to sing. Mrs. Fleischman had a beautiful smile on her face combined with a look of approval, tapping her foot in time with the song. She was astonished with the sound.

"I never expected to hear the quality, the tone, the blend of harmony that I am hearing. It sounds like there's an orchestra in this room. Who taught you how to harmonize, like this?" asked Mr. Fleischman.

"It was Larry," Paulie replied, "He gave us our sound."

"Who taught you Larry?" asked Mr. Fleischman.

Larry was confused by the question. "I don't really know, Mr. Fleischman. It just seems to come to me. There's a certain sound I want to hear and I know it when I hear it."

Mr. Fleischman complemented Larry. "Larry, you are a natural, you are blessed. It's a gift. You are all blessed. Keep up the good work and may God bless all of you. Mazel tov (which means good luck and blessings in Yiddish)." Everyone said their goodbyes and were about to leave, when Johnny turned to Mr. Fleischman and announced to him, "By the way Mr. Fleischman I am a Shabbats Goy, and if I could be of any assistance, please sir, don't hesitate in giving me a holler."

Mr. Fleischman responded, "Thank you Johnny. I'll keep that in mind."

Shabbats Goy means, a Gentile for the Sabbath. Once the Sabbath begins on at sundown on Friday an Orthodox Jew can't perform any kind of a manual chore and that includes turning on or off light switches, turning off gas jets etc. A Shabbats Goy could perform these little things for any religious Jew that would ask.

{ 11 }

The following day, Larry was standing by his shoeshine stand in front of Izzy's Barbershop when a beautiful young African woman came walking by. He noticed her passing by in the past but never had enough nerve to talk to her. She was always carrying books, and she always looked as though she didn't want to be bothered. But this time Larry thought, aah, what the hell? What's the worst that could happen? So, he called out, "Hey mama. How you doin'? Don't I know you from somewhere?"

The lady stopped in her tracks, turned slowly, faced Larry and in a beautiful soft toned, very eloquent voice, with a wonderful accent, responded, "First of all, I am not your mama, and is that the way you address a lady?"

Larry was embarrassed and became all tongue-tied, "No-no, I didn't mean to insult you. It's just the way we talk around here."

Lady: "You can talk whichever way you choose to talk around here, but you don't speak to me in that manner!"

An embarrassed Larry responded, "I am so very, very sorry if I insulted you. Please forgive me and accept my apology."

The young lady accepted Larry's apology, then stated, "You see, you can be a gentlemen!."

Larry asked, "I always see you carrying so many books. Are you a schoolteacher?"

The lady responded, "No, I am an exchange student from Nigeria attending New York University majoring in education and for now, I am living with an aunt."

Larry, with his ignorant innocence, "Nigeria, where is that? The only Nigeria I know is the falls"

The young lady chuckled, "No that's Niagara. Nigeria is a country on the African continent. And where are you from?"

Larry replied, "Oh, I'm from Harlem."

The young lady chuckled again, "No, where are your ancestors from?"

Larry replied again, "Oh I don't have any aunts, and I don't have any sisters."

She chuckled once again while thinking that Larry is kind of cute, "We all come from somewhere else," she explained to him.

"I gotta look into that, yeah I gotta look into that. By the way, my name is Larry and what's yours?"

"My name is Abeo."

Larry repeated her name, "Abeo, that's a pretty name. Does it have a meaning?"

"Yes Larry, it has meaning. It means, to bring joy."

Larry thought to himself, "I can sure see you bringing me joy, a whole lot of joy."

Larry and Abeo conversed for a while before she had to leave. Larry hoped that she could stay longer but didn't want to push the issue. She told Larry that she must leave because has a whole lot of studying to do for an upcoming test. He then mentioned that there was going to be a dance on Saturday night at the community center and that he would like it very much if she would come to hear his group perform.

Abeo hesitated for a moment, giving it some thought, "Okay, I think I would enjoy that very much. I've been studying very hard lately and a little time off would do me good. I'll try my best to make it."

Needless to say, Larry was thrilled and couldn't wait for Saturday to arrive.

{ 12 }

Now that the group was going to be making their debut appearance they needed to be outfitted. This meant going shopping on Orchard Street. Everybody went shopping on Orchard Street for clothes, shoes, jewelry, and much more. It was a shopper's paradise. Even people from the neighboring states would go shopping on Orchard Street because of all the great bargains.

Orchard Street was about five blocks long and had dozens and dozens of stores and pushcarts. Almost all of the merchants, if not all the merchants, spoke Yiddish and English as well, and were of the Jewish faith. It truly had the old world flavor. Businesses on Orchard Street were open six days a week, closed on Saturdays, the Jewish Sabbath, and reopened on Sundays for business as usual. Johnny, being a Catholic, could never understand why the Sabbath was changed from Saturday to Sunday for the Christians. He believed, as he was taught, that when God created the world, he rested on the seventh day, which in all actuality, is the last day of the week, and the last day of the week being Saturday should be the Sabbath for everyone. Johnny felt that the Jews had it right.

Paulie mentioned to the guys that if they waited until Sunday to do their shopping there was a good possibility that the bargains would be even better. He let the guys in on a little secret telling them that a lot of the merchants believed that if they made a sale on the first customer who entered the store that day, the rest of the day and week would be very profitable. Knowing this, you were able to bargain with the merchant for a cheaper price on the merchandise you were buying. As far as the merchants were concerned, they had to make that first sale.

The guys in the group all had black pants and white shirts. All they needed were matching ties and a sports jacket. They hit the store just right. At least, that's what they thought. They discussed price with the merchant and the merchant told them that the jackets that they were interested in were $30 apiece. The guys told the store owner that they could afford $15 for each jacket. The merchant raised his voice and asked the guys to leave. On the way out the door the merchant said "All right. I'll give you the jackets for $25 apiece."

Johnny replied, "All we can afford is $15 each for the jacket!"

This went on for a while. The salesman in a high-pitched voice, with a heavy Yiddish accent and a face turning red as a tomato said, "Get out, get out, get out, you're making me crazy."

Trying to keep a serious face once more, all the guys turned to leave the store. The salesman called them back and said, "Okay, okay, you win give me $20 each. Take the jackets and leave."

Georgie Mo said to the merchant, "Sorry we took up so much of your time. We'll get out of your hair and leave."

With that, the merchant rolled up four jackets, put them in individual bags, stuck out his hand and said, "Give me the $60 for four jackets and now get out."

The guys walked out with four sports jackets, regular priced at $30 each, for $15, along with matching ties, for a buck a piece, and left the shop thinking they made a great deal. They were so proud of themselves for how they handled that deal until they passed the store next door to where they bought their merchandise and saw the same jackets in the window for $15. Be careful what you bargain for. You might just get it. Orchard Street is not the same today. The stores are high end. There is no bargaining, and it has lost that old-world flavor. What a shame!

{ 13 }

Back in the 1950s, drugs weren't as predominant as they are today. There was pot and heroin, but gangs weren't battling over the drug trade and blowing one another away to gain control of the drug trade in their neighborhoods. There were plenty of gangs in the New York area and there were plenty of gang wars usually over something petty like coming into one another's turf (neighborhood), or who the tougher gang was, or blaming someone for looking at my girl, and nonsense like that. If you got caught up in a gang fight that was unexpected, you grabbed anything around you to defend yourself because the gang that you were fighting usually had sticks, bats, knives, and sometimes, unexpectedly, a zip gun (a homemade gun). You could grab anything you could get your hands on quick like a garbage pail cover, a car antenna ripped from a car and used as a whip, or really anything that would cause considerable damage to one's anatomy; and of course, your fist and your feet.

From time to time, one gang member would challenge another gang member to a fair fight. This was called a fair one. No one from either gang would jump in at any time and the only weapon was your fist.

If two gangs were planning to go at one another, each gang had a warlord and the warlords would meet to determine the location and the weapons to be used. Then you had the kids who weren't gang members, but knew how to defend themselves, and defend themselves well, if there were any problems with some of the gangs.

The majority of kids from the stoop were great kids that had their heads screwed on and never looked for any trouble. Johnny, Larry, Paulie and Georgie were these type of kids. No one messed with Johnny Gun. Everyone knew his reputation for being tough if he had to, but all they wanted to do was sing and have fun. Everyone knew that at the upcoming Saturday night dance some gang members would show up, and as long as they were there to dance with their own girls, and act like gentlemen, there wouldn't be any problem. Even the gangs during that time had respect!

By the way, the gangs were made up of all different nationalities and races. There were Spanish gangs, Italian gangs, Irish gangs, African-American gangs, Chinese and multi-ethnic gangs. The gangs came from all parts of the city. And why were there so many gangs? It was, as I mentioned earlier, how people of different ethnic groups were learning how to live together while still having fears of others because of the lack of understanding for the different races, nationalities and traditions; all creating these pocket neighborhoods.

Chinatown was a very closed society to outsiders, except for their fabulous Chinese restaurants. What went on in Chinatown among the Chinese, stayed in Chinatown. There was plenty of crime in Chinatown with the Chinese gangs, and that's where it stayed.

Most all this frivolous behavior was conducted by the youth gangs. You also had adult gangs, but they weren't considered gangs at all. They were known as businessmen, illegitimate businessmen, specializing in organized crime such as gambling, shylocking, prostitution, and of course, back in the 1920s...bootlegging, just to mention a few of their *business enterprises.*

Every neighborhood had its bookies and its shylocks. A shylock was someone you could go to to borrow money from for a very high rate of interest. Or, you could go to a bookie to place a horse bet or to bet the numbers.

The numbers racket was very simple. All you had to do was to place a bet on a three digit number that would come out in the daily news every evening after the racetracks would close. They took the number from the last three digits of the total mutual handle, which was all the money the racetrack handled that day. It paid 500 to 1 to the winner of the bet. So, if you placed a 25-cent bet and hit the three digit number, you would receive $125 dollars back.

I would venture to say 50% or more of the neighborhood people would play the numbers, and most of the people who played the numbers were the working people. Although it was against the law, the people wanted to bet the numbers. This was the most popular betting at the time before New York started the lottery, but even today with the lottery, the numbers racket continues. The winnings are tax-free!

That's enough about gangs and organized crime. This was just another insight into the daily goings-on in the neighborhood as in many other New York neighborhoods.

{ 14 }

Carmen's career was really taking off. She was packing the house at the Greenwich Club in Greenwich Village every night. Johnny was becoming a little concerned with their relationship. Would this new found success that Carmen was experiencing destroy their relationship?

One night after Carmen's show, Johnny showed up at the club to walk Carmen home. Carmen noticed that Johnny looked a little down and was kind of quiet.

She asked Johnny, "Sweetheart, you look a little out of it this evening. Are you all right? Is there something wrong?"

Johnny, with a soft tone to his voice replied, "I'm not sure. Will you always love me no matter how successful you become? Could anything come between us?"

At that point Carmen shared a story with Johnny that her mother had shared with her. "Sweetheart, I asked my mother why she left show business. She sat me down and discussed the pros and cons of the business. Like myself, she loved to sing, but there was an upside and a downside to the profession. The upside, of course, was the love for music and the love for singing. The downside was when it started to become a business and she started to feel like a piece of property, an object for managers, agents, and PR people. It was like they were tugging at her from all sides and that's what she couldn't deal with. It was then that she had a choice to make. And until this day, she is not sorry for the choice she made. There were two things she was not willing to give up; her independence and the love she had for my father. As far as she was concerned, my mother would never allow anything to come between them. All of these years, she let my father believe that it was he who prevented her from going into show business."

Before Carmen had a chance to say another word Johnny says, "Sweetheart you said it all. I thank you and I love you."

Eventually, something similar would happen to Carmen. Working in nightclubs wasn't what Carmen really expected. In time, she realized how much of a homebody person she was. Dealing with drunken patrons that were sometimes abusive, Carmen knew that she would never get used to that lifestyle. The art of singing is one thing. That's easy to love, but the business that goes along with it can sometimes make for a very unhappy lifestyle.

It was kind of ironic that Carmen's mother and Johnnie's mother were both singers and their children were following in suit. Kids have a tendency of taking their parents for granted, and Johnny was no different. Johnny heard his mother sing all his life. He knew she was a good singer, but never realized how good.

Johnny and his family were invited to a wedding of a friend's daughter. Like at so many weddings, people who knew how to sing, and even those who didn't know how to sing, but liked to sing, would be invited up to the bandstand. The bride's mother and father were good friends with Johnny's parents, and they were aware of how good of a singer Johnny's mother Antoinette was, especially when she sung in Italian. So naturally, they asked her to sing.

At weddings or functions, whenever Johnny's mother was asked to get up and sing, Johnny would escort her to the stage. His mother started to sing a beautiful Italian song while Johnny waited in the wings to escort his mother back to her table when she was done singing. When Antoinette started to sing, a crowd gathered around the bandstand. Johnny took notice of the crowd and watched as a little Italian man pushed his way through the crowd to get close to the bandstand. As he stood in front of the bandstand, this gentleman raised both hands up in praise to Johnny's mother with undying approval and tears running down his face.

Johnny always knew that his mother was a wonderful singer, but now realized, for the first time, how many hearts she was touching and how this went beyond just singing. Johnny's mother always told him to never turn his back to an audience and to never forget that when you sing a song, sing it like you are telling the audience a story, something that a singer must always be mindful of. She also explained to him that a voice and song should be like a beautiful marriage. The song should complement the voice and the voice should complement the song. One should never outdo the other. So here we have Johnny's mother, Carmen's mother, Paulie's father, all good singers, even Mrs. Bentley, who was still singing with her church choir as she's been doing for many years, having their children come together to carry on a tradition, and that is a love for singing.

Well what about Georgie Mo? Where did his voice come from? Georgie and Johnny both attended Catholic elementary school where they were both altar and choirboys. Despite the fact that Georgie was a big pain in the ass, he was also blessed with a beautiful voice. Until he was about 13 years old, Georgie stuttered but never when he would sing. He was an angel with a dirty face.

One night Georgie was sitting on the stoop waiting for the guys and the rest of the crowd when Frannie happened by. "Say something stupid to me, Georgie Mo, and I'll punch you all over the street."

More than anyone else in the crowd, Georgie would tease Frannie the most. He loved to get Frannie's Irish temper all riled up. In his own dopey way he would get a kick out of it when she got mad. He thought she was cute, but never gave her any indication or anyone else, for that matter, that he had a little crush on her, and you would never think it. This particular night was a little different, or should I say, a lot different, for our buddy Georgie Mo and Frannie.

He stood up, looked into her eyes and said, "Yeah, yeah, yeah, you think you're a tough girl. You wanna punch me all over the street, but what if I held you so tight that you couldn't move?"

Before Frannie had a chance to do anything or say anything Georgie followed through, by grabbing her, holding her tight around her arms and kissing her square on the lips. Fran managed to push him away. She looked into his eyes like she was going to hit him, but instead, grabbed him like he was a rag doll and kissed him square on his lips. Thus began a romance that would last a lifetime.

Larry, who was sitting on the stoop, looked up in amazement and couldn't believe what he was seeing and responded in his high spirited comedic way, "My, my, my, one never knows. Does one?"

{ 15 }

When Johnny and his family moved into the Williamsburg section of Brooklyn, he began meeting a lot of good guys who also became very good friends. Four of the guys had a vocal group called the Splendors, and they were good. Johnny told them about the dance at the settlement house on the Lower East Side and asked them if they would like to come and do a few songs. They agreed.

Every neighborhood in Brooklyn, Manhattan, Queens, the Bronx, and Staten Island and beyond, had doo-wop groups. It was the sign of the times, and the times were great with music pouring out from all over. They sang about love. They sang about going steady. They sang about breaking up then making up. It was a great era for music, and it was the beginning of rock 'n roll. It was like so many other eras of the past when the kids had their own music. It was beautiful and it was great.

Georgie had heard about another great group who came from the East New York section of Brooklyn and were working a lot of the clubs all over the New York area. The name of the group was the Bari Trio. This particular night they were working a club in Ridgewood

Queens. The Bari Trio was a little older, which meant they were more experienced and a lot more professional than the younger groups around at that time. Georgie suggested to Johnny, Paulie, and Larry that it would be a good idea to catch their show, there could be quite a bit they could learn. The Bari Trio wasn't a doo-wop group. They all played instruments. When the guys heard them sing they were amazed with their voices, with their showmanship, and how they held an audience in the palm of their hands, especially with their humor. They were singing classic tunes that never go out of style and they were great. They were all magnificent guys with super personalities and it showed when they did their comedy. They were superb.

Johnny knew, and the rest of the guys knew, that they had to introduce themselves to the Bari Trio and get to know them, which they did. When the trio finished their set, Johnny and the fellows introduced themselves and asked if they could do an acapella doo-wop song the next set. The Bari Trio agreed and the next set, Harmony, went on the stage. They did one song and got a good response from the audience. After the trio's last set, Mike from the trio stayed to talk to the guys of Harmony. One of the many things Mike discussed with Harmony was when they're on-stage they should always remember to sing for the audience, respect the audience, and have a good time. If you're having a good time, so is the audience.

Mike became a good friend to Harmony, and he told them that if there was anything he could do for them, to just give him a call. It was a great evening for the guys and very memorable for them. It was really the first time they sang in front of an audience as a group. They also had the pleasure of meeting and learning quite a bit from a great group, the Bari Trio.

The five boroughs of New York had many bar lounges. Some of the lounges were owned by connected guys (affiliated with organized crime). You could feel very comfortable and safe going into any one of these lounges and be assured that no one would ever get out of hand with you or your lady. If someone was foolish enough to step out of line with anyone in these establishments, it was assured that they got their head handed to them and that was that.

There were more characters in the New York area, I believe, than in any other place in the world; characters that were so naturally funny with humorous situations taking place on a daily basis in their lives. This is how so many of the great comedians got their material for their careers.

Mike D'Bari, from the Bari Trio, had told Harmony a funny story about a bar in Brooklyn that was on a triangular corner. It had three entrances, one facing east, one facing west, and one facing south. One of the patrons got very drunk and began causing a ruckus. The bouncer picked him up by the collar and threw him out. The drunk went around the corner and came in the other door and, once again, he got thrown out. He went around to the other entrance which was the East entrance. When approached by the bouncer for the third time, the drunk looked at him and said, "How many bars do you guys own on this street?" They all laugh their heads off and the owner bought the drunken guy a steak dinner, but no more alcohol!

{ 16 }

The neighborhood had its array of characters that could have stepped right out of central casting, like *Tony Swag*. Swag is a word that was used for hot or stolen merchandise. It had a proper meaning, but the street guys would take a proper word and change its meaning to whatever they wanted it to mean. It was their language that they all understood.

Tony was a well-liked guy who would give you the shirt off his back or the tie from around his neck. Anyone who admired the tie he was wearing got that tie. He was a superb dresser and always looked sharp. Anything you needed Tony had, and anything you wanted, Tony could get. He had a dry sense of humor. He was a natural comedian. Tony was Johnny's cousin.

One day Tony called Johnny to tell him to come over to his apartment and try on a pair of very expensive Italian made shoes, swag of course. Johnny asked Tony the size of the shoes. Tony told Johnny that they were a 10 ½.

Johnny stated, "I'm not a 10 ½, I'm an 11, 11 ½, depending on how the shoe is made." Tony told Johnny, "Come over and try them on, anyway. The shoe is like butter. You never know. They might just fit."

Johnny went over to Tony's apartment to try on the shoes. He put on one of the shoes and his toes were all scrunched like an accordion.

Johnny told Tony, "I knew they wouldn't fit Tony. They're too tight."

With this, Tony responded in his very dry comedic sense of humor, "Try the other one on."

Anytime Johnny would tell that story, people would crack up laughing. When the group went to buy their matching jackets for the show, Tony had nothing on hand. He gave them all a beautiful pair of Italian-made shoes as a gift, and this time they all fit.

Then there was *Crazy Willy*. Don't get confused with the name. He wasn't crazy. He was just extremely funny and made everyone else crazy and did a lot of crazy things, some of which we cannot speak about.

Somehow, Willy got involved in the funeral business. The wise guys in the neighborhood wouldn't shake hands with Willy anymore. They believed it was bad luck to shake hands with anyone who was in the funeral business.

Willy started carrying a measuring tape in his pocket. He took the tape wherever he went, affairs, nightclubs like the Copa, the Latin Quarter, wherever he would go. When the guys weren't looking, he would stand behind them and measure them. Then he'd tell them that he had a casket size to fit all of them. They were very superstitious, and he knew this would make them crazy.

You see, guys like Willie, Tony Swag, everybody in the neighborhood, including the wise guys, their girlfriends, or their wives, heard that Johnny was putting together a group and they couldn't wait to hear them. Johnny was well-liked in the neighborhood by everyone, even the wise guys because of all the respect he had for all people. The whole neighborhood, and I mean the whole neighborhood, became very supportive of the group and couldn't wait for the Saturday night dance. This is how four young guys, a Jew, an African American, an Irish Italian, and a Polish kid, didn't even realize they were bringing a neighborhood together to trust one another regardless of their different religions, different races and nationalities. They were actually saying, look at us, we're doing it.

The neighborhood folks would also have bragging rights. Every neighborhood, at that time, had some sort of a celebrity or a doo-wop group. In a quiet way they would compete with one another. This was Harmony's time to shine. This, indeed, was becoming the neighborhood's biggest event. They were four good kids and everybody wanted the best for them. This was going to be Harmony's neighborhood debut, and the excitement was running rampant.

The Bari Trio offered to play behind Harmony for the dance and would be the house band for the night, at no charge. How blessed the guys felt that the neighborhood people were so supportive in coming together for them. The group felt more excited about doing this show than they felt about the upcoming citywide doo-wop competition. Harmony was beginning to mean more than just the name of a vocal group.

{ 17 }

The day of the dance finally arrived. Harmony and the Bari Trio got together in the early part of the afternoon for a final rehearsal and a sound check. After the rehearsal they all got together and were treated to lunch at Molinski delicatessen, Georgie Mo's father's place. For the rest of the afternoon all the guys just hung out, relaxed, shared stories with one another, and had a lot of laughs before the adrenaline rush and the pre-show jitters set-in. The doors were scheduled to open at 7:00 PM and people were beginning to line up as early as 5:00 o'clock.

Finally, it was show time, and the joint was jumping! It was a packed house filled with people from all over the neighborhood and beyond. Different clicks came from all parts of the city including Brooklyn, Queens, and the Bronx. Everyone was dressed to the hilt. When an event is about to take place the news travels fast and far. Everyone knows someone who knows someone. A lot of vocal groups with their following were coming to check out this new group called Harmony. You see, these were some of the groups who were competing with Harmony at the citywide competition, and they wanted to see and hear who they were going up against. Mothers, fathers, aunts, uncles, cousins, and friends; neighborhood people who lived in the same neighborhood for years and who had never met, finally came together for the first time. They were all in attendance. Once again, Harmony was becoming more than just the name of a vocal group.

The Bari Trio kicked off the night and the party got under way with people dancing all over the place. Sitting in with the Bari Trio, that evening, was a good friend of Harmony, a Puerto Rican kid from the neighborhood. They called him Joey Conga. Joey was part of a Latin band that played most of the Latin dances throughout the city. He played the Conga drums. The Conga is a standup drum that you play with your hands. Joey was the best of the best.

The doors to the settlement house were wide open. The music, the rhythm, the beat was heard throughout the neighborhood. People were dancing in the street. No one was complaining about the noise so the cops didn't have to be called. And anyhow, Johnny's mother and father were in attendance and Johnny's father was a police sergeant.

Harmony was scheduled to go on at 9:00 o'clock. The group from Brooklyn, the Splendors, which Johnny had invited to do a few songs, would sing first. Some of the other groups at the dance asked if they could sing.

Without any hesitation, Johnny, Larry, Paulie, and Georgie Mo welcomed them to do so. They were all fantastic. They were the competition, but now they all became friends with deep respect for one another. All the other groups and their following, who also came to the dance, started seeing Harmony as a bunch of great guys.

Johnny asked Mike D'Bari to have Carmen get up and sing a song. Carmen knew nothing about this.

Mike D'Bari gets on the mic, "And now ladies and gentlemen, we have a special guest in the audience. A young lady with a magnificent voice. I give you Lady Latina herself, Carmen."

Carmen was not expecting to sing that evening. Needless to say, she was beside herself. Johnny took Carmen by the hand and whispered in her ear, "Sing Carmen, please sing! Tonight sing for your mother and your father!" And that she did. This evening would also be an evening of joyful tears and proud fulfillment especially from the parents. Carmen's mother was holding back her tears with a beautiful pleasant look on her face. Carmen's father was another story.

With tears streaming down his face he whispers in Manuela's ear, "The last time a woman sang to me like that was some 20 years ago. She is truly her mother's daughter."

Larry was kind of nervous at the beginning of the evening, but it wasn't because of the show. Abeo promised that she would come that evening and Larry was hoping that she didn't change her mind. When she came walking into the dance it seemed as if Larry saw no one but her.

Larry greets Abeo, "I'm so glad that you could make it. I thought of nothing but you since that day we met."

"I thought about you, Larry, and I thought about you a lot. I wouldn't have missed your debut for nothing," Abeo told Larry.

Then there was Frannie who came to the dance with a few of her friends from Brooklyn. They were the same girls who came to visit her in the neighborhood to meet the crowd. Frannie knew that one of the girls, Flora, had a crush on Paulie from when she first saw him, so Frannie reintroduced Flora to Paulie.

Frannie walked over to Paulie, "Paulie, did you meet Flora?"

Paulie, viewing Flora from head to toe, "Yes, but I was never formally introduced."

Paulie was that classy type of a guy who believed very much in protocol. Paulie greeted Flora, "Hello Flora. It's very nice to meet you."

Flora returned the greeting to Paulie, "And it's very nice to meet you Paulie."

Paulie asked Flora where she was from. "I'm from the Ocean Parkway section of Brooklyn." Flora responded.

Paulie sporting a curious look on his face asked Flora, "Are you Jewish?"

Flora smiled, "Yes Paul, I am Jewish."

Paulie with a big smile said, "So am I."

Back then, most Jews, as well as Catholics, would marry within their faith for religious reasons. One of the concerns for the families of a mixed marriage, that is, a Jew and a Catholic, was which faith the child be raised in. For some families it mattered very much, and for some families it wasn't as much of a concern. In all religions there are those who practice their religious traditions and there are those who don't. It doesn't mean they don't believe in a higher power. They believe wholeheartedly in God, but choose to practice God without following any religion or religious denomination. This was not the case with Paulie and Flora. They were both Jews who believed very much in following the Jewish faith as reformed Jews. In short, Orthodox Jews are the most observant and stringent with no variations from Jewish law. Conservative Jews are more flexible, leaving out some laws difficult to follow in modern times. The reformed Jew is even more flexible, dancing and singing during services, and no requirements for dress, shorter services, and mixed marriages. As the writer of this book, I dated a few Jewish girls in my teen years. I thought I was very much in love with one girl until that time came when she respected her family's wishes and started dating a real nice Jewish fellow whom she later married. Growing up in a very diversified area, I learned about others and their traditions, and learned to respect them.

Now let's get back to that evening's festivities. Vivaciously, Mike D'Bari introduced the guys. "And now ladies and gentlemen, the pride of your neighborhood, direct from their stoop, and straight into our hearts, I give you Harmony!"

As Harmony took the stage, cheers went up, along with screaming and applause. One by one the group came onto the stage to take their positions. With heads bowed, hands clasped low and in front of them, they waited for complete silence. Finally, there was not a sound in the auditorium. With complete silence in the auditorium, letting a few seconds pass, they began. In a very high pitch, but soft velvet tone, the indication of not just a good singer, but a great singer, Paulie delivered his first note. Johnny, Georgie Mo, and Larry gave Paulie the perfect background harmony, all using their voices like perfect instruments. The family, the friends, and acquaintances, and the entire audience seem to be taken to another dimension, another world, a magical world, created by the sounds coming from these four beautiful voices, these four beautiful kids. They sang for over an hour. They sang some of the songs of the day and also some of their original songs to the delight of the hundreds of people attending this event and they were perfect. If I were to say they were great, it would be an understatement.

Paulie shared with the guys whatever he learned about voice taught to him by his father Cantor Fleischman that enhanced their voices considerably. That evening, they did more for the audience than entertain them with a magnificent show. Four young guys, each being of a different religion, different race, and different nationality were making a statement and didn't even realize they were doing so. They were showing the neighborhood, that it wasn't that difficult to respect and get along with one another, regardless of their differences. Yes, I'll say it again. **HARMONY** was more than just a name of a vocal group.

After the group finished their performance they left the stage to be surrounded by the audience that wanted to congratulate them and let them know how wonderful they were and how surprised the audience was with the group's magnificent sound and performance. A few black dudes approached Larry and questioned him about why he was singing with three white guys.

Paulie overheard the conversation and intervened, "What does it matter who sings with who as long as you can get the perfect sound? Or maybe you guys, knowing and hearing how good Larry is, maybe you would wish he was singing with you. Could that be?"

With that, the black dudes smiled, shook Larry and Paulie's hands, wished them luck, and told them how much they enjoyed Harmony, then left.

It was a beautiful evening in more ways than one. The weather was perfect. There was a full moon and the magic of romance was in the air. Taking their girls by their hands, they proceeded to walk down to the East River Drive and walk along the river, which, to them, was the most romantic place in the world.

Manhattan Island is bordered by two Rivers, the Hudson River to the west and the East River to the east. Crossing over the Hudson River was the George Washington Bridge connecting New Jersey to Manhattan. Crossing over the southern part of the East River were three bridges, the Brooklyn Bridge, the Manhattan Bridge, and the Williamsburg Bridge, which connected Manhattan to Brooklyn. Going further north, the East River flowed into the Harlem River. The guys with the girls walked along that part of the river that had the Williamsburg Bridge in the foreground. With the river and the bridge all lit up, and the moon reflecting off the ripples of the river, the entire evening was just a beautiful and a most memorable one. It couldn't have gotten any better than that.

The weeks that followed were dedicated to rehearsals and hard work in preparation for the citywide doo-wop competition that would give the winners a shot at stardom and a recording contract.

{ 18 }

After the night of the dance, four neighborhood stars emerged. The guys were having a ball with all the attention they were receiving in the neighborhood. Four young boys about 11 years of age, who were listening in from the outside of the dance, approached Larry and asked Larry to teach them harmony.

Larry was more than willing when Georgie Mo stepped in and said, "Allow me".

Larry's responded, "Of course Mo. Georgie is going to give you young fellows a lesson in harmony."

Georgie proceeded in teaching the little guys the same way that Larry taught him and Johnny. Larry got the biggest kick out of watching Georgie give a lesson in harmony to four wide-eyed kids, also of different ethnic backgrounds.

The high Jewish holidays were approaching while the guys were preparing for the citywide doo-wop competition. Paulie's father, Cantor Fleischman, became ill and would not be able to perform at the holiday services. The elders of the synagogue approached Paulie to ask him if he would fill in for his father at the holiday services. Paulie knew that this was the right thing to do, but the time of the service would conflict with the citywide competition. Paulie turned down the elders because of the commitment he had made first with Harmony.

One night, when all the guys and girls were sitting on the stoop, Mrs. Horowitz, from her window asked Paulie, "How is your father feeling? I understand that the Cantor won't be able to perform the holiday services." The guys were very concerned and asked Paulie if his father was going to be all right?

Paulie responded by telling them, "My father has been working very hard lately. The doctors told him that he was suffering from exhaustion among a few other physical problems, and it was imperative that he rest to avoid any future complications."

Johnny asked Paulie, "What about it Paulie. Are you able to fill in for your father?"

Paulie answered, "I made a commitment with Harmony, and I'll fulfill that commitment. I won't let you guys down."

The guys looked at one another knowing what each one was thinking at the same time. Georgie Mo responded, "You dummy. We thought you knew better than that. A family member needs help, and you put that aside for something secondary. I'd like to bang you around and drive some sense into you. I speak for all of us when I say, "What you've done is unacceptable and out of order. What kind of friends would we be if we didn't put first things first? We won't have it. You go and fulfill your obligation to your father and your Temple and you better sing your ass off or I'll kick your ass. Now get going and straighten out this matter."

With tears in his eyes at that moment, Paulie realized he had the best of friends in the whole world; friends that became family and a relationship that would last a lifetime.

{ 19 }

It was evening and Johnny, Carmen and the rest of the crowd, except for Georgie Mo and Larry, were sitting on the stoop when Mrs. Bentley came running down the block. Johnny asked Mrs. Bentley what was wrong. In a very frantic tone, Mrs. Bentley told Johnny that Pop's Candy Store was held up and pop was beaten so bad that he was in a coma. She told Johnny that there was an eyewitness who pinned Larry and Georgie Mo as the assailants. Johnny ran to his father's station house and asked his father what was going on. His father told him that an eyewitness saw Georgie Mo and Larry enter the candy store about the time the incident occurred.

Johnny frantically told his father, "Dad, Georgie and Larry would never do such a thing. It has to be some kind of a setup, a mistake. It's impossible, Dad. I tell you; it's impossible."

Johnny's dad promised to do everything possible to get to the bottom of all of this. Meanwhile, Johnny and Paulie went all over the neighborhood trying to get information, but no one knew anything. Paulie told Johnny to get some sleep so they could start out early in the morning to get more information. Johnny told

Paulie, "There is no way possible, Paulie, that I'll get any sleep tonight knowing that these two guys are locked-up for something we know they didn't do."

The next morning Johnny was getting ready when his phone rang. At the other end was Frankie V, a good friend of Johnny, who owned a luncheonette on 9th Street.

Frankie V asked Johnny, "Johnny, I understand that you have two friends who were accused of sticking up Pop's Candy Store and putting pop in the hospital?" Johnny was surprised to hear from Frankie, "Frankie, did you hear anything?"

Frankie V proceeded to tell Johnny that the night before he was getting ready to close when a bunch of wise asses came in for coffee. He overheard them bragging about a robbery they did in a candy store. Johnny asked Frankie if he knew who these guys were, and where they were from. Frankie told Johnny that from time to time they came in. Frankie told Johnny, "I know they have a club on 11th Street and Avenue C. I hope that can help you Johnny." Johnny thanked Frankie, and told him how much he appreciated the call. When Johnny met Paulie that morning, he told Paulie where he had to go and what he had to do. Paulie insisted that he go with Johnny. Johnny told Paulie that he's just going up to the club to talk and get more information. But Paulie knew better. He knew that Johnny was gonna put his life on the line to save his friends.

Johnny arrived at the club and knocked on the door. The door opened and Johnny pushed his way into the club. "I understand you might have some information for me pertaining to the stickup at Pop's Candy Store. Who's the president of the club, I wanna speak to the president?"

A big wise ass stepped out from the back room, "I'm the president. Who the fuck are you and what do you want?"

Johnny viewed him from head to toe, "What's your name?"

"Bouncer. They call me bouncer cause I bounce people around," the president responded.

Johnny, soft spoken but pissed off, said, "If you don't give me the information I'm looking for, I'm goanna kick your ass and bounce you from wall to wall."

The Bouncer, thinking he's enlightening Johnny responded, "There's six of us and one of you. How do you intend to do that?" With that Johnny hit the bouncer in the mouth, then picked him up, got behind him and put him in a choke lock.

"Who beat up Pop and robbed his candy store?"

The other five guys that sat around the club all stood up to go after Johnny. Just then the club door got kicked open and in came Paulie, Frannie and Frannie's six brothers. Needless to say, the club members took one hell of a beating. They beat the hell out of the club members and proceeded to wreck the club while Johnny had the bouncer in a chokehold and wouldn't let go until the bouncer gave Johnny the information he was looking for. The bouncer must have known that this guy Johnny meant business as he started to spill his guts, giving Johnny the information that would clear Georgie Mo and Larry. They turned the bouncer over to the police. By that time, Pop came out of his coma and fingered the bouncer as his assailant.

{ 20 }

It was the High Holy day and Paulie was at the synagogue preparing for the services. Growing up in an area with so much diversification, you seem to become so much a part of the environment, so much a part of who you're living with. Any major holiday, whether it be a national holiday or a holy holiday, the air is filled with a certain excitement. A special day during the calendar year, whether it be a national holiday or a holy day, there's a certain feeling that some of us experience, even though it may not be a holy day of our faith.

All the Jewish ladies and gentlemen in the neighborhood were dressed in their holiday best. Even some of the non-Jews would dress up in respect for their Jewish friends. This was the case with Paulie, Larry, and Georgie Mo. The guys were hanging out on the stoop all dressed up in their Sunday best, waiting for the services to begin so they could walk over to the synagogue, to hear Paulie sing. The synagogue was going to be packed. The doors would be wide open making room for the overflow of parishioners and, of course, there was no air-conditioning. The door to the apartment house opened and out stepped Mrs. Horowitz, who was very elegantly dressed.

Georgie Mo looked up, and to everyone's surprise, instead of teasing Mrs. Horowitz, as he usually did, he commented, "Mrs. Horowitz, you look stunning. May I have the pleasure of escorting you to the synagogue?"

Mrs. Horowitz, poised in a very dignified manner, replied with that beautiful Yiddish accent, "Yes you may, but watch yourself baby. I'm one hell of a tough old broad and don't bother asking me to make mad passionate love with you. I'm not that type of a girl. Now let's get on with it."

With that, Mrs. Horowitz took Georgie by one arm. Frannie took Georgie's other arm, and together they go strutting down the street toward the synagogue. By this time, the congregation was gathering. As expected, there were people on the inside and people standing on the outside of the synagogue. The crowd quieted down as services were about to begin. Paulie began to sing. He sings a wonderful song called *Koll Nadre*. There is not one word of that song that I understand, but every time I hear it an unexplainable, magnificent feeling comes over me. Without knowing what it means, the feel of that song, and the person singing it brings me to tears. The only other song that even comes close for me is *Mendelssohn's Ave Maria*.

The guys looked at one another and could not believe what was coming out of the mouth of this little skinny Jewish guy with big black rim glasses, red hair, and ears that made him look like a taxicab coming down the street with the two backdoors open. Was he a beautiful guy? You bet your life he was, and all the girls thought he was exceptionally cute.

{ 21 }

After the services Johnny, the guys, and the rest of the crowd from the stoop discussed how many times they heard Paulie sing and had no doubt he had a great voice. But this day his singing today was not only great, it put him in a class all by himself, a class of his own. He was extraordinary!

Georgie Mo turned to Frannie, "I had a lot to do with Paulie's superb performance today!"

Frannie questioned, "Why? Cause you taught him how to sing?"

"No. But I told him to sing his ass off, or I would break his ass."

With much sarcasm, Frannie looked into Georgie's eyes and said, "You're magnificent. What would people do without you?"

Someone happened to mention the time. It dawned on the guys that if they would hurry, they might have time to make the doo-wop competition. One of the guys in the neighborhood had a car and offered to drive Harmony. They all piled in and headed uptown to the theater where the competition was being held.

This was not just a show-up that day competition. All applicants had to apply by mail six-months prior to the competition. The competition date fell on the same day as Passover, making a possibility for a conflict of time. Knowing this, Harmony had gotten in touch with the competition committee and asked if they could be the last group to compete that day. Thankfully, the committee had approved it.

Even with this forethought, they still were not sure if they would make it in time.

There were 50 groups competing. By the time Harmony arrived, they were up to number 40. The guys had made it with time to spare! Harmony listened intensely as each group performed their songs.

"These groups are fantastic," Johnny told Larry.

Larry replied, "And so are we!"

Up against this level of competition, and believe it, the competition was stiff, the fellows now had a barometer to indicate how they measured up in the doo-wop world. Some of the groups performing had very good lead singers, but none had a lead singer as good as Paulie. Some groups were better with the up-tempo tunes, which they preferred to do, and some would prefer the slower tunes. Harmony did both very well, but no one did a slow love song like Paulie because Paulie respected a song and sang each song as though it was holy. This was taught to him by his father, Cantor Fleischman.

Their adrenaline was pumping. They just couldn't wait to get up there on the stage and just sing, something they loved to do more than anything. You see, they viewed singing as a joy. Because they loved it so much, they had fun with it. At this point, winning or losing didn't matter to them. All they wanted to do was to try their best and enjoy what they did together; to sing their hearts out. It didn't really matter what anyone thought of them. Harmony's biggest thrill would prove to be their debut performance at the settlement house and being able to sing for their neighborhood.

It was their turn. They took the stage and that's exactly what they did. They sang their hearts out. Many members of the other groups applauded Harmony, approached them and congratulated them after their performance. They met some of the groups before at the community center dance.

It was time for the winner to be announced. Harmony came in second. There were five judges, four male and one female. They were all affiliated with different areas of the music business. After the winner was announced, one of the sound engineers came over to Harmony and said, "Something is wrong here. You were the best group on the program. Something is not right!"

Harmony took what the engineer said with a grain of salt and left the theater. They didn't win. To them, second place wasn't bad. It was still a good position, especially, for a new group.

{ 22 }

A few days later, Johnny was at home with his mother and father having dinner when there was a knock at the door. When Johnny opened the door a gentleman introduced himself as Steve Norris, an independent record producer who was at the theater for the competition. He wanted to speak to Harmony, but in all the confusion when Norris turned around, Harmony had left the theater. Johnny asked Steve to come in and meet his mother and father. Antoinette, Johnny's mother, cordially invited Mr. Norris to join them for dinner.

Steve apologized for interrupting their dinner. "Thank you Mrs. Shea. I appreciate that very much, but I have a dinner engagement this evening."

Norris told Johnny that he got Johnny's address from one of the sound engineers. He wanted to discuss a recording contract for Harmony. He told Johnny he wasn't sure how legit that competition was, but he knew what he heard from Harmony. It was great, and he wanted to record Harmony, if the group was interested. Mr. Norris asked Johnny to please discuss it with the group and get back to him as soon as possible. With that, Johnny ran out of the house to gather-up the guys to tell them the good news.

As expected, Larry, Paulie, and Georgie Mo, were elated. Back in the 1950s, the record industry was a lot different than it is today. A lot of the neighborhood groups from around the city would go up to Sanders Recording on Sixth Avenue, which was a small 10 x 10 storefront recording studio. The guys would pay their $10 and record a song, acapella (voices only, no background music). They would then take copies around to all the small independent and major companies in the area.

The building, located at 1650 Broadway Avenue, was loaded with a lot of independent record companies, always looking for new talent. If you were lucky and had a good product, you were signed to a recording contract. Some of the artists' dreams would come true, a few, very few. The majority of artists searching for their dreams were turned away. That didn't stop some who got turned down from pursuing a career in show business. Many of them became very successful in their pursuit. Harmony was fortunate being in the right place at the right time with a producer taking notice of their talent. Their time had come, and they were ready to record.

Steve Norris, Harmony's producer, had given the group two songs on a tape that he wanted them to record. The guys worked for hours, practicing the two new songs. They had no idea what a recording session would entail, having never recorded in a major recording studio.

The boys arrived at the studio in uptown Manhattan at 7:00 AM. The musicians would also have gotten the songs weeks in advance to prepare for the recording session. Harmony began rehearsing with the musicians. They rehearsed for hours until everything, the sound, the music, the voices, were to the producer's satisfaction.

Steve Norris was a marketing genius in the recording industry. He knew what would sell, and he knew what the public wanted. He wouldn't settle for anything less.

It was time to record what they worked on for weeks and what they rehearsed with the musicians for hours. The sound engineers, the A&R people, who were to do the recordings, took sound checks of everyone's voices and the musical instruments for a perfect blend between the music and the voices.

The actual recording began. There were many takes. The recording session went on for hours and it would only end when Steve Norris had his product just the way he wanted it. Harmony had arrived at the studio at 7:00 AM and finished recording at 1:00 AM the next morning.

Norris was pleased knowing that he had a hit record and a hit group. Harmony was very tired, but not too tired to be ecstatic to hear the play backs that they created with all their hard work.

Weeks went by and the guys hadn't heard from Steve Norris. They tried calling, but hadn't received a response. They left messages with Steve's secretary, but he never got back to them. The guys were very anxious to know when their recording was going to hit the airwaves, if indeed it would. They had no idea what was going on and how long it would be, if ever, before their record would be heard on the radio.

It was a beautiful Saturday afternoon and Harmony, along with the whole gang, were hanging out, on and around the stoop, doing what they normally do, socializing and having a good time, laughing, joking, and teasing, as usual. Larry was across the street tending to his business, shining shoes in front of Izzy's Barbershop, while his girlfriend, Abeo, was sitting on the stoop admiring Larry from afar. Georgie Mo and Paulie Red were leaning up against a 1958 Chevy schmoozing with their girlfriends, while Johnny was waiting for Carmen to come down.

Johnny was wondering how long it was going to take Carmen to come downstairs, when suddenly, Carmen's window to her apartment flew open as wide as it could be opened. A radio was blasting from Carmen's apartment loud enough for the whole block to hear, and what they heard was their dream come true, the voices of Harmony and their first recording playing across the airwaves. For any singer or singers it is a thrill of a lifetime to hear your recording played on radio for the first time and your voices introduced to the public. If all goes well, this could just be the beginning of a successful singing career; a dream-come-true for the guys. Needless to say, this was a thrill, not only for Harmony, but also for their friends, their families, and the whole neighborhood. To think the whole gang from the stoop and the entire neighborhood had four of their own, singing on the radio and becoming celebrities.

About an hour passed, and guess who came into the neighborhood? It was their producer Steve Norris! Steve was greeted by the guys with excitement and wonder.

An ecstatic Johnny said, "This is fantastic, Steve. This is fantastic. We tried calling you many times, but you never got back to us. We were wondering if everything was alright."

Steve told the group, "I was very busy promoting your record to all the radio stations. I didn't want to get back to you with false hope or any excuses until I nailed it, and we did just that. Every radio station in the tri-state area and beyond will be playing your record. They love you and want to hear more of you. In a few weeks, I'm sending you fellows on tour to promote your record."

{ 23 }

It was Friday evening and the guys were scheduled to leave for their promotional tour the following Monday. They decided that they wanted to do something special for themselves and the girls on Saturday. They decide that Saturday afternoon would be a good time to have a good old fashion stickball game. Different neighborhoods had stickball teams, so they got in touch with one of the teams from one of the neighborhoods and planned a stickball game that Saturday afternoon.

Stickball was a game you played with a Spalding rubber ball and a stick. The stick was a broom handle or a mop handle. Many kids got in trouble with their mothers for sawing-off the head of a broom or a mop to play this game. Some teams would play for money, and some teams would play for bragging rights. This game was for beer and to have a little fun. The losers would buy the beer, and the winners, in most cases, would share it with everyone. So everyone drank, whether you were a winner or loser.

The guys also planned a surprisingly wonderful evening with the girls. Everyone was out in the neighborhood watching and enjoying the stickball game, while the girls were on the stoop wondering what the surprise would be that evening. The game ended with Harmony losing and everyone was drinking beer, bought by Harmony. As I already mentioned, back in the 1950s, in New York, the drinking age was 18.

Arrangements were made for the four couples to meet on the stoop at 7:00 o'clock. 7:00 o'clock came and everyone was there dressed in their finest. There were two taxi cabs with two couples in each taxi, and off they went uptown. The excitement was building as the taxicabs pulled up in front of the world famous Copa Cabana nightclub on 10 E. 60th Street where Johnny Mathis was appearing that evening. Needless to say, all of them were star struck. It was a wonderful evening. For the first time, everyone was experiencing a nightclub and listening to the magnificent angelic voice of Johnny Mathis. The next day, being Sunday, no one was in a rush to get home. Once again, romance was in the air as the four couples went back to their most romantic place in the world, the East River Drive along the East River. With the backdrop of the full moon and Williamsburg Bridge all lit-up, it was one romantic evening.

Abeo asked Larry for a favor, "Larry, when you find the time, will you promise me that you will get your high school diploma?"

Larry, in all sincerity, made her that promise that evening, and eventually, would do more than just a high school diploma.

Johnny reminded Carmen about their conversation concerning Carmen's mother and why she didn't pursue a career in singing. He let Carmen know that he was going to keep a sharp eye on how he was treated by managers and record company moguls.

Georgie Mo and Fran were getting in as much hugging and kissing as they possibly could, knowing that it would be a while before they could hold one another again.

Paulie left the stoop earlier in the evening. He got on the D train going to Brooklyn, getting off at Church Avenue, making sure that Flora got home safe to her home on Ocean Parkway. It was a wonderful evening, but also kind of a bitter sweet one, knowing that they wouldn't see one another for a month or so.

{ 24 }

It was a dreary Monday morning. The skies were overcast and there was some drizzle. The boys arrived at the Brill Building on Broadway to meet up with their bus transportation and other recording artists who were going on tour promoting their new record releases. The record company's policy was to send their artists out on the road, making public appearances to promote their artists, as well as their records. Depending on the length of the tour, this could become very trying and hard work for the entertainer. They would spend many nights doing one night stands, changing clothes in a bus and grabbing something to eat on the run. This would go on until they reached their next destination where they would be put up in motels that were not the best of motels. In the South, the white entertainers would sleep in motels for whites only and the black entertainers would be segregated in a hotel for blacks only.

This was the fifties and much of that nonsense was still going on. The guys never figured on this. They were in for one hell of an experience. This was explained to Larry by his mother, so Larry had a good idea of what to expect but never mentioned it to any of the guys.

Everyone got along well on the bus, laughing, joking, getting to know one another, and sharing experiences. Some of the artists on the bus were already star celebrities who had taken a few of these tours. A lot of friends were made. Harmony found it hard to believe that they were part of this, and in the company of some of their favorite recording artists.

Their first stop was a three-day Rock N' Roll show in Ohio, in a theater with over 2000 screaming kids. Ohio wasn't a segregated state, so the audience of black or white could sit wherever they wished. This was a blast for Harmony. This was a dream come true, so they thought. They were four young, good-looking guys getting more attention from the audience, especially the female audience, then they could have never imagined.

How do young kids handle this tremendous amount of attention without getting a fat head? You can see why so many entertainers, especially young entertainers, become ungrounded and develop a loss of reality, as they fall right into the clutches of all the hoop-la. It's not easy to be put on a pedestal, especially the young, when they receive so much praise and get looked up to as some sort of deity. They developed into someone or something they're not, apart from normal society. The bigger the celebrity status, the more some of them forgot who they really were and where they were from. Could this happen to Harmony? Maybe so, but let's see how their new experience would change them for the better, or not.

The next stop was below the Mason Dixon line where segregation was in full bloom. It started to get a little peculiar to Johnny, Georgie, and Paulie when the bus made a dinner stop at a cafeteria that was segregated. Johnny asked, "What the hell is that all about?"

One of the black entertainers on the bus explained that this is the South, and in the South, segregation is a part of life. Whites don't eat with Negroes and Negroes don't eat with whites. Slavery was abolished, but there was no equality.

"Does that mean that Larry has to separate himself from us when we go to eat?" Johnny asked, with a rebellious tone of voice.

Larry tried to tone it down by saying, "That's okay fellas. It was explained to me years ago by my mother. I understand."

Georgie Mo was pissed off and added, "That is bull shit. This is all a lot of crap. We can't have dinner with one of our friends? It sounds like a bunch of nonsense to me."

Larry tried to enlighten Georgie Mo, "Nonsense yes, but down here, it's a fact."

Paulie spoke up, "I don't like this, guys. I just don't like it! And we gotta live like this for how long? What about our sleeping arrangements? The same bullshit?"

Back on the bus some of the black entertainers who became friends with Harmony noticed that the guys had a change of attitude. They seemed to be very down and they were very quiet not understanding why this sort of thing had to exist. In their neighborhood, and in surrounding neighborhoods of the Lower East Side, different nationalities and different races were sometimes frowned upon, but no one had to eat in separate sections of restaurants. This was a whole new experience of life for the guys, and there was more to come.

That night they arrived at the motel, but it wasn't a motel for everyone. This establishment catered to whites only, while the black entertainers spent that evening at a motel for blacks a mile away. That was all that the guys had to see. The next day Johnny didn't ask, but told the tour manager that Harmony, from now on, would be sleeping and eating on the bus as one. We would use these small minded establishments to shower etc., but we refuse to be separated under these conditions. The tour manager told Johnny that he couldn't allow that to happen.

With that, Georgie Mo approached the manager and read him the riot act. "Not to mention any names, you've been banging one of the female singers on tour with us. Does your wife know about this? I'm sure she would understand, wouldn't she?"

The tour manager was dumbfounded, and the guys got just what they wanted. The boys discussed this segregation thing amongst themselves and hoped that someday things would change for the black folks of the South.

As they went on from city to city, town after town with the show, they became less enthusiastic on stage as they looked out into a segregated audience. This was far from the excitement they experienced at their first show in Ohio.

Traveling the South they saw many things like separate drinking fountains, separate bathrooms, separate waiting rooms. In laundromats they saw separate sections, even for washing your clothes. This was completely unacceptable for these four guys from New York. You're talking about four kids who came from a low income society that didn't have much in way of material things, but were able to go anywhere in their city that they chose to go to and appreciate all the simple things in their lives and in their environments.

It's true that different nationalities and different races had their own neighborhoods in New York City, but in time, this would thin out, making most neighborhoods accessible to all who were willing to establish themselves there. Yes, to them the South was America, but not a free America, as they experienced in everyday life from where they came.

{ 25 }

The tour ended with great reviews. The audience loved Harmony and loved their songs. They met a lot of people and signed a lot of autographs. The record company was already planning another tour. How did Harmony feel about all this and what did they think about this new experience that came into their lives?

The record company assigned a public relations firm to the group. Their job at the time was to market the product. In this case, the product, being Harmony, was to appeal more to the public.

The PR people, as they were known, would promote the artist, as well as the record, to the general public. They would ask for some background information of the artist and beef it up, sometimes to a point that would be tilted and not the truth, to make the artist appear a lot different, a lot bigger than life than he or she actually was. In public they were told what to say, how to act, and even what to wear. Sometimes it would be an improvement for the artist, but sometimes if the artists didn't need much improvement, they had to do as they were told by the record company.

Like a lot of the movie companies back in the 1930s, 1940s and 1950s, their actors were their products. Some of them were told what to eat, when to sleep, how to look, etc. They became a product of the movie companies.

So many solo artists and vocal groups made peanuts in comparison to what the record companies and half-ass managers were making off them. It was like selling your soul to the devil for a little fame. As good as a lot of these artists were, many of them never received the recognition and the money that they well deserved.

For all of you young artists today or those of you, who want to become part of the entertainment industry, don't be blind to the fame and glamour that you are seeing through the media. Go behind the scenes and research what it really entails to become part of the world of entertainment. Never forget that there is always more than meets the eye. What is really behind the glamour is much hard work and sacrificing. That's why you really have to love the business. Be smart. Don't be fooled, and never let anyone take away your true identity.

Harmony was beginning to feel the pressure from the record company and all that went along with being a success in the recording industry. Johnny remembers the conversation that he had with Carmen pertaining to Carmen's mother and how she gave it all up for a normal family life instead of a professional life in show business. When the guys were traveling the South, Larry was willing to accept all of this nonsense that went on in the South. He repeated to the guys many times that the way he was being treated was all right, and he was willing to make the sacrifice for the rest of the group, even if it meant giving up his equality for their chance at the big time.

Johnny, Paulie, and Georgie Mo sat Larry down one evening after the tour and Georgie Mo began speaking for the group, "Yes Larry, we appreciate all that you want to do for us and we love you for it. We also know, for the sake of the group, that you would never tell us how much it hurts you. But we are sitting down, right here, right now with you, to let you know how much we feel the hurt for you. You say to us, it's all right, guys. It's all right, I can accept it. But, we say to you that although you can accept it and you say it's all right, we can't accept it, and will never accept it, and it is definitely not all right with us. When we see one of ours being treated like a low-life, a second class citizen, it hurts us. It hurts us bad."

Larry realized that all they were saying was sincere and absolutely how they all felt. Larry realized that he couldn't deny the guys' their true feelings. This was also a good time for Harmony to discuss their future.

{ 26 }

"Well, we've seen and experienced what it's all about. What do we really think about it?" asked Johnny.

Paulie answered, "As I see it, you have to be a certain type to get involved with show business. You have to be willing to give up the family lifestyle as we know it, having to spend a lot of time on the road and away from our family and friends."

Paulie asked Johnny about his feelings and his thoughts. Johnny said, "When we were away, in my quiet times, my thoughts were about so many things, a lot of little things like stickball, punch ball, singing doo-wop. I very much missed Carmen, all of our friends, and family, the neighborhood, and our stoop. I knew we found our home, and it wasn't on the road. It was always there, where we just came back to...the stoop."

With a look of approval, Larry added, "Johnny, you're speaking for all of us, and the little things you spoke about, well then, they ain't that little! They mean everything and so much more to all of us."

Georgie Mo chimed in with that dopey looking facial expression, "I missed all that too, and I can't believe I even missed my father's deli."

Johnny explained, "What we've done and what we've experienced in such a short time, allowed us to discover the really true treasures and what is most valuable and most precious in our lives. We had to travel half of the country to realize this, but as we look back, it all worked to our advantage."

{ 27 }

The families were so happy when the guys returned. Johnny's mother decided that she was going to make a dinner for Harmony, their families and their girlfriends. Mrs. Shea was a great cook.

As always, after dinner, when guests came to Johnny's home, there was singing and a lot of it. Everyone was amazed when Cantor Fleischman sang an Al Jolson tune, *Rock a Bye Your Baby*. Paulie shared how his father would sing beautiful love songs to his wife, Mrs. Fleischman. How beautiful is that?

Mr. Molinski, Georgie Mo's father, pulled out a harmonica from his jacket pocket and started playing tunes that everyone was able to sing along with.

Mrs. Bentley, who always sang with her church choir, sang a song, *God Bless the Child*, that she would dedicate to her son Larry, Johnny, Paulie and Georgie Mo.

Carmen's mother, and Johnny's mother, Antoinette, did a duet. They performed a beautiful love song that Manuela would sing in Spanish and Antoinette would sing in Italian.

The English version of the song is called *You Belong to My Heart (Solamente una Vez)*.

Johnny's father, Patty, was a good father. He would do what most good fathers would do. He threw Johnny his first baseball, taught Johnny how to ride a bike, and brought Johnny to his first baseball game and many after.

He did for his children what a good father would normally do. As a husband, coming from that male dominant society, as so many men did, they cared more about their emotions and their feelings. Some husbands gave their wife little or no respect as a wife and a human being. At times, it almost seemed that the wife was a second-class citizen and not an equal. This was the case with Johnny's father. When he would drink he would become verbally abusive and sometimes physically abusive. This went on for years. One day Johnny's mother, Antoinette, was conversing with her mother in Italian about how she was being mistreated. She got slapped in the face by her mother and was told to go home and take care of her husband. Talk about the old foolish world! Johnny and his sister, Marie, saw this going on for years.

Marie, who was two years younger than Johnny, never forgot how every Christmas Eve, her father would come home from work drunk and be abusive to their mom. Marie and Johnny would always be fearful of Christmas Eve, especially Marie, because of the way their father acted when he would drink.

One evening Johnny was at his cousin's house when the phone rang, and it was Marie. Johnny's cousin gave the phone to Johnny.

Marie said in a forceful tone, "Get home. I just beat the shit out of our father."

Johnny couldn't believe what he was hearing, "What happened, Marie?"

Marie replied in disgust, "I can't take it anymore, and I won't take it anymore, our father coming home drunk and lifting his hands to our mother. I slapped him around, threw him in bed, and undressed him."

Johnny and his cousin Tony arrived at Johnny's home and looked at one another in amazement. Antoinette, Johnny's mother, was sitting at the kitchen table with tears in her eyes but a look of relief on her face as to say, finally, something was done. Antoinette felt terrible that it had to come to this. But words were never enough for Patty, Johnny's father. Understand that Marie was daddy's pet, his little angel.

Johnny told Marie, "If I would have done what you did to daddy, he would've looked for me with a baseball bat to break my legs."

Who would have thought at that time, that a 16-year-old girl with a magnificent passive personality could have straightened out a man who was the way he was all of his life?

The next day was a Saturday, and Marie and Johnny stayed very close to home to see what their father's reaction would be. Well, there was no violent reaction. On the contrary, peace buzzed through the railroad apartment like never before. Marie asked her father if he remembered what happened the night before. He had no words, no animosity, and a look of complete shame on his face. From that day on, there might have been some arguing from time to time, but never verbal abuse or physical abuse. Mama finally got her equal rights that her daughter was more than willing to fight for.

While everyone was having a good time at the dinner party, Patty, Johnny's father, would normally sing, but this time he did something altogether different. From his jacket pocket he took out a piece of paper with writing on it and said, "I wrote something that I would like to read, if it's okay with my family."

Marie, "Of course daddy, please!" Patty begins to read:

IF I WERE TO CHOOSE AGAIN
(A FATHERS PRAYER)

I COULD NEVER SAY AS SOME DO WHEN THEY SAY
IF I HAD TO DO IT ALL OVER AGAIN I WOULDN'T
CHANGE A THING
IT IS TRUE THERE ARE CERTAIN THINGS I WOULDN'T
CHANGE
BUT IT IS ALSO TRUE THAT THERE ARE SOME THINGS I
WOULD WANT TO CHANGE
IT I WERE TO CHOOSE AGAIN

IF I WERE TO CHOOSE AGAIN

THE HURT AND THE PAIN THAT I HAVE CAUSED TO SO
MANY
WOULD BECOME THE HAPPINESS AND LOVE, THEY SO
MUCH DESERVE

IF I WERE TO CHOOSE AGAIN
THE SELFISHNESS THAT I HELD ON TO
WOULD BECOME THE CARING HEART FOR OTHERS
FOR THEIR FEELINGS AND FOR THEIR SITUATIONS

HOW HAPPY IT WOULD MAKE ME
IF I WERE TO CHOOSE AGAIN
TO GIVE SO MUCH MORE OF MYSELF
INSTEAD OF TAKING ALL OF WHAT THEY WERE SO
WILLING TO GIVE

DEAR LORD
IF I WERE TO CHOOSE AGAIN
I WOULD TRY WITH EVERTHING I HAVE
NEVER TO HURT OR LET DOWN A SINGLE SOUL
ABOVE ALL LORD
THY WOULD BE DONE
WITH YOUR HELP PLEASE ALLOW ME LORD
JUST ONE MORE TIME JUST THIS ONCE TO
CHOOSE AGAIN

After Patty's reading, there was complete silence for about 10 seconds and not a dry eye in the house. Cantor Fleischman approached Patty, puts his hands on Patty's shoulders and said to Patty, "Patty my newfound dear friend, you are truly a man of integrity to share that beautiful writing with all of us."

{ 28 }

One day, even before this story began, Johnny and Georgie Mo were hanging out just doing nothing, when Georgie began rattling on about how dirty the Lower East Side was with dog shit in the streets, bubble gum stuck all over the sidewalks, garbage pails overflowing with garbage, the smell of cats pee, and he kept going on and on.

Johnny told Georgie, "Georgie, you're missing something. You're looking at it optically. You're not seeing what this neighborhood is all about. You're not looking into the heart of this neighborhood and what makes it tick. It's all about people, our friends, families, your family, my family. It's what we talked about in the past. It's about hard-working people, good people, strong people, who are breaking their backs giving everything they got, struggling, trying to make it in life to create something good for themselves and their families. They have pride, loads of pride. The people are the pride of the Lower East Side.

This city, this vast metropolis, didn't sprout up on its own. It was built by men, immigrant men and woman, to become the center of the world, the whole world in one place, and so many of them coming from the Lower East Side. Yes, the neighborhood might look ghetto, but its people are not. So stop your babbling and take a good look."

At this point, the guys were all satisfied with their experience in showbiz and wanted more than ever to go on with their lives.

The Vietnam War came along. One day Larry announced to the guys that he was joining the Army. Georgie Mo and the guys were surprised to hear Larry's plans. Larry explained to the guys how he made a promise to Abeo that he would get his high school diploma, and going into the Army would help him fulfill that promise.

Georgie Mo, as usual, had to break balls, "Of all the stupid things I ever heard, only a jerk would give themselves up to get shot at just for a high school diploma. What a dope!"

Larry laughed it off and said to Georgie, "One of the things I'm gonna miss most, Georgie, is your open, very subtle personality, and all that goes along with it!"

Georgie hugged Larry and whispered in his ear, "Take good care of yourself, you fool, or I'll break your ass."

With that, all the guys hugged with tears in their eyes as they sent Larry off.

{ 29 }

Some time passed, and Johnny, who really never wanted to become a cop like his father, began to reconsider. Johnny spoke to Carmen and told her his plan.

"Honey, I'm considering taking the exam for the New York City Police Department. Whatta you think?" asked Johnny.

Carmen replied, "I think I'll love you, no matter what choice you make. How about that?"

Johnny took the test and passed it. He entered the police academy for his training and began to feel like he made the right decision. It's the perfect profession for one who embraces justice and wants to protect the little guy. That's Johnny's profile in a nutshell.

Georgie Mo, naturally, had something to say, calling Johnny a flat foot with a flat ass and big tree stumps for arms and always telling him, "Be careful you don't catch a bullet in the ass". Yet, he knew that Johnny would make a great cop.

Paulie stayed in the neighborhood and in a short while became Cantor of the same Temple as his father.

Larry came home on leave after his basic training and greeted Johnny and Paulie on the stoop. Not seeing one another for some time, they really enjoyed the time they spent together.

Larry informed the guys that he received his high school diploma. Now the Army was sending him to school to become a medic. The guys thought it was great to see how Larry was progressing, but were worried about Larry going to Vietnam.

Georgie Mo came walking down the block to the stoop. He had a very peculiar look on his face, one that none of the guys have ever seen before. They hugged and were all happy to see one another.

Johnny questioned Georgie, "What's up kid? Are you all right? It looks like you're a little troubled. Is something bothering you? What's up?"

With a solemn look on his face, Georgie Mo replied, "My draft notice came today."

Johnny, Larry and Paulie were surprised to hear about Georgie's draft notice. Holding back their laughter, Johnny and the guys were going to get their chance to break balls on Georgie Mo.

Paulie began, "Does the Army realize who their getting? The prize that they have chosen to join them and all the magnificent gifts and talents that come along with him? You make me proud, Georgie, that I could sleep safe and sound every night knowing that the great Georgie Mo is looking after all of us. Thank you God, thank you God!"

Johnny injected, "Watch yourself, my dear friend, and be very careful not to take a bullet in the ass. We know that it's not a possibility, but just in case, our prayers are with you, always."

Larry put his arm around Georgie and announced to him, "And if you do catch a bullet in your ass, I, Lawrence Bentley III, will be there to put a Band-Aid on your wound and send you on your way with love."

"Never, never, never! I will never catch a bullet in my ass," Georgie Mo replied.

Time was up and Larry had to leave, but before he left, he had another announcement, "Oh, and by the way, fellas, Mrs. Bentley sends her love."

"How is mom? Don't forget to send her our love. We hardly see her. We really should go visit her," Johnny promised.

With a sly look on his face, Larry said, "That's not the Mrs. Bentley I'm talking about."

Georgie Mo was confused. "What Mrs. Bentley are you talking about? We only know one Mrs. Bentley?"

Larry smiled, "Abeo Bentley, my wife."

Paulie surprised, "You and Abeo are married? When? Where?"

Larry replied, "Abeo came to see me on visitor's day and we both made the decision to do it then. She'll be coming with me to my next duty station while I train in the states."

At first, the guys' reaction was that they couldn't believe this was happening. When it finally sunk in, there was much joy and jubilation.

Georgie Mo reminded Larry, "Now, don't go getting yourself killed. There's a wife you have to come home to and a bunch of guys who love you very much. So don't do nothing stupid or I'll kick your ass."

{ 30 }

Two years passed and Larry had returned from Vietnam. Working as a medic in the Army, Larry realized his forte. He gave it a lot of thought with Abeo's encouragement in becoming a doctor. Larry always had the brains to do great things. All he needed was someone to ignite his fire. That he got from his loving wife, Abeo, who, by the way, began teaching school.

One day, Johnny ran into Frannie on the Avenue. Frannie told Johnny that Georgie Mo would be coming home soon. She told Johnny that on the last day of his deployment in Vietnam he got wounded and you would never guess where. Johnny was concerned about the wound and how fatal it was.

Frannie told Johnny, "Don't worry Johnny. It wasn't life-threatening. They sent him to a hospital for a few weeks, and now he's on his way home. I'll let him tell you about his million dollar wound."

Johnny felt relieved and said, "Wait until I see that bum. This is something I'll never let him live down."

Johnny informed Frannie that he and Carmen were getting engaged.

Frannie said to Johnny, "You two guys have been doing everything together since you were kids and this is no different. Georgie and I are also getting engaged. Are we looking at a double wedding?"

Two weeks later, Johnny and Paulie were sitting on the stoop when, suddenly, who turns the corner limping down the street? You guessed it, Georgie Mo, back in the neighborhood. Johnny and Paulie greeted him and welcomed him back.

"How was it over there?" Paulie asked Georgie. In all sincerity, Georgie told the guys, "You're not going to believe this, but I really missed the deli."

In a sarcastic tone, Johnny said, "I noticed you were limping a little coming down the block. Are you okay?"

Georgie told Johnny that he bumped his leg on a chair when leaving his apartment.

"Oh. I understand." Johnny replied. "Come over here. Sit on the stoop and relax."

Georgie told Johnny that he'd rather stand. Johnny kept edging Georgie on to sit knowing that Georgie couldn't sit because of his wound. Johnny insisted that Georgie was hiding something and wouldn't tell us what it was.

Johnny insisted, "Come on Georgie. Is there something you want to tell us?"

Georgie whispered to Johnny and Paulie, "I took a bullet in the ass."

Johnny said to Georgie in a loud tone of voice, "I can't hear you. Please speak louder."

Georgie Mo finally gave in with a loud voice, "All right you ball breakers. I took a bullet in the ass!"

Johnny looked at Paulie, laughing their heads off. "We finally did it Paulie. We finally got even with the neighborhood ball breaker, the great Georgie Mo. What a great feeling; something that will go down in history."

Georgie asked where Larry was and how Larry was doing. When Johnny told Georgie that Larry was going to college and had plans to become a doctor, Georgie's response was, "I knew that kid had something special in him. He didn't fool me for one minute. I'm proud of that dope."

{ 31 }

So it was. Johnny and Carmen are married and living in Brooklyn with their two loving children. Johnny became high-ranking in the New York City Police Department and never regretted becoming a cop.

Paulie had followed in his father's footsteps and became a Cantor. He and his beautiful wife, Flora, and their three children, one boy and two girls, are living in a beautiful condo on the Lower East Side.

Georgie Mo's parents left him the deli. Georgie took the family's recipe for sausage and parlayed it into a national phenomenon making Georgie a millionaire. Georgie and Frannie are married with six children and are living on Long Island, New York.

Dr. and Mrs. Larry Bentley III are living in a section of Harlem called Sugar Hill, a very high-end area with their two children. Larry kept his promise to his mother. Mama Bentley was treated and lived like a Queen until her death. Larry and Abeo spend a few months each year in Nigeria tending to the medical needs for the poor, free of charge.

{ The Reunion 2019 }

After sitting on the stoop for three hours reminiscing about their lives together growing up on the Lower East Side, someone got a brainstorm. "Hey, let's play a little stickball."

By this time, all of their wives, Abeo, Carmen, Flora, and Frannie, joined them. The plan was to have dinner together after the guys were done discussing their plans for the Gateway Arts Foundation, the non-profit musical foundation for the neighborhood kids. The foundation would pay for their lessons, so the kids could fulfill their musical dreams. There is so much talent in this neighborhood and the guys want to help these kids cultivate their talents. It's like the old generation helping the new, giving back to a neighborhood that gave them so very much. Harmony had many friends that were more than willing to help the Foundation raise whatever money was needed for their success.

Georgie Mo announced to the guys, "I'm rich. I got your backs. Name it and it's yours." Georgie never had much class, but you gotta love him.

When Frannie, Georgie Mo's wife, heard someone suggest a stickball game Frannie's response was, "This, girls, we have to see. I wouldn't miss this for the world. Get the hot tubs and the horse liniment ready for our aging men!"

Some kids were on the block playing stickball, and the guys asked if they could challenge them. The kids looked at one another not knowing how to respond to four guys who were in their 70s. The kids were very cordial and very respectful and agreed to the challenge.

First, second, and third base were already made in the street with chalk. You play the game the same way you play baseball. Either someone pitches the ball to the batter for the batter to hit, or at least tries to hit, or the batter throws the ball up and tries hitting it himself, then runs the bases. The idea, of course, is to try to get a hit. You're allowed two swings. If you miss, you struck out. (The kids today are still using the same type of rubber ball and stickball bat made out of a mop or broom handle, just like we did back in the 1950s).

And the games began. The first-inning: three strikeouts for the guys, no hits. The kids: 15 hits, 11 runs. Top of the second inning for the guys: three strikes you're out, no hits. The wives were having a ball cheering on their men and hysterically laughing at the same time.

Georgie Mo yelled out to his wife, Frannie, "You think you can do better?"

Frannie grabbed the bat from Georgie, "Alright, kid. Put one over the plate."

The first pitch, Frannie hit a pop fly that was caught. She looked at Georgie and said, "At least I hit one."

The girls cracked-up laughing. The game ended there, and thank God for that, before someone got a heart attack or pulled out their back trying to hit a little rubber ball. At that age, the mind wants to do so much, but the body doesn't agree.

What Harmony was about to do was a great contribution for kids on the Lower East Side. This was a very special day for the guys and their families. This was the pinnacle of their lives, to be able to help so many city kids who had untapped talents that might have gone unnoticed. This is how it began for Harmony, four kids with no formal training in the arts and so much untapped talent, that were given a chance.

Mr. Driscoll, of the Parks Department, was the gentleman who was in charge of many of the free venues and events that took place throughout the city. Mr. Driscoll was planning an event, a concert that would take place on the East River Drive, a great park located on the Lower East Side along the East River where the guys and girls used to stroll. The concert would consist of singers, rappers, and dancers.

After speaking with Mr. Driscoll about the scholarship program, Mr. Driscoll immediately became an advocate and a friend of the program.

Mr. Driscoll invited Harmony and their families to the event to announce their plans for starting a foundation that would help the kids from the Lower East Side who were interested in pursuing a career in the musical arts.

This type of event would be very new and very different for Harmony. Harmony would never limit themselves or be closed minded to any good talent as long as it was good clean fun. They were always willing to give kids a chance.

At that time, the park had an amphitheater where the actual event would take place. The area was packed with participants and a huge audience. The entertainment was great. The singers, the dancers, the rappers performed their rhythmic poetry and kept it very clean. The guys and their wives were amazed and impressed with all this untapped, magnificent talent. What these kids were doing was art.

Mr. Driscoll took the stage and asked for a little quiet because he had an announcement to make. Mr. Driscoll called for attention, "Kids, this evening I'd like to introduce you to four fantastic guys who grew up right here on the

Lower East Side. In their day, back in the 1950s, they had a great singing group and traveled a lot of our country entertaining and singing their hearts out. They are with us this evening to share with all of you a new, free program, if you qualify. The program will help those who are interested in, and who have a love for the arts, or anyone considering the arts as a profession."

Mr. Driscoll went on to explain what the program was all about and if anyone wanted any more information, there were flyers available. He then announced, "Maybe with a little bit coaxing, we can get these four fellows up to do some acapella singing for us." The audience applauded as Harmony took the stage.

Paulie spoke for the group, "Some 50 years ago four young guys came together not knowing one another to form a singing group. We called ourselves Harmony, a name that would take on more than just the name of a vocal group. It became a name that would join us together in love and friendship for the rest of our lives and bring a neighborhood closer together. For all of you young people, we would like to share something with you that became very important to us. In choosing a profession of any kind, take time and make sure that you are not choosing a profession just for the money or the celebrity status. Sometimes you can become a rich, but a miserable, unhappy individual.

Choose for the love of whatever it is you wish to pursue. When the hip-hop and rapper craze came along, I wanted to try my hand at writing a little rap poetry. I came up with some words that would describe the Lower East Side and its beginnings. So please let a bunch of 70-year-old guys join all of you as we give it our best shot. It goes something like this."

Georgie Mo leans over to Paulie, "You wrote a Rap song. A holy, Jewish Cantor writes a Rap song? You should be ashamed of yourself. That's a sacrilege!"

Paulie whispered in Georgie's ear, "Like my father said many times, and as I said many times in the past, any song is a holy song as long as you sing it from your heart, you dummy!" Georgie was shocked to hear Paulie calling him a dummy. Imagine the great Georgie Mo being called a dummy. What was this world coming to?

Paulie told the guys, "Whenever I give you the queue, I want all of you with loud voices to say, THE PEOPLE ARE THE PRIDE OF THE LOWER EAST SIDE, and encourage the audience to do the same. I'll start. Ready 1, 2, 3, 4. After the first line, a bass guitar player started to give the rap a great rhythm, a great tempo. Hook that up with all the hand-clapping, and it was Harmony once again.

GET ON BOARD ALL YOU MY FRIENDS

GONNA TAKE YOU FOR A RIDE – WHERE THE CULTURE
NEVER ENDS
GONNA TAKE IT NICE AND EASY – GONNA TAKE IT REAL
SLOW
GONNA TAKE YOU FOR A RIDE TO THE LOWER EAST
SIDE

GOD HAD A PLAN – NOT HARD TO UNDERSTAND
TO LIVE AS ONE TO WORK HAND AND HAND
FROM AROUND THE WORLD – FROM FAR AND WIDE
HE BROUGHT THEM ALL TOGETHER TO THE LOWER
EAST SIDE

SO WHO IS THE PRIDE OF THE LOWER EAST SIDE
THE PEOPLE ARE THE PRIDE OF THE LOWER EAST
SIDE

IN TENAMENTS AND PROJECTS THE PEOPLE CAME TO
LIVE
THEIR REASON FOR SUCCESS IS WHAT THEY HAD TO
GIVE
THEY GAVE OF THEMSELVES, THEIR HEARTS AND
THEIR SOULS
THEY'RE THE SAME TODAY AS THEY WERE IN OLD

SO WHO IS THE PRIDE OF THE LOWER EAST SIDE
THE PEOPLE ARE THE PRIDE OF THE LOWER EAST
SIDE
I SAID – WHO IS THE PRIDE OF THE LOWER EAST SIDE
THE PEOPLE ARE THE PRIDE OF THE LOWER EAST
SIDE
THE STREETS WERE KINDA MEAN FOR THOSE WHO
DIDN'T CARE
THEY MADE THEIR LIVES TOUGH – THEY DIDN'T WANT
TO SHARE
SHARE IN THE WORK OF EVERYDAY LIFE
LOOK FOR THE EASY WAY OUT
CREATING NOTH'IN BUT STRIFE

BUT ALL AND ALL THEY WERE JUST A SMALL PART
OF A NEIGHBORHOOD THAT HAD SUCH A VERY BIG
HEART
THE HEART OF A PEOPLE WHO HAS SO MUCH PRIDE
THEY ALWAYS WERE AND WILL BE FROM THE LOWER
EAST SIDE

171

RENOVATE – CULTIVATE, THESE THINGS ARE TAKING
PLACE
BRINGING FORTH THE BEAUTY, CLEANING UP THEIR
FACE
THEY TAKE IT ALL IN STRIDE, THERE'S NOTH'IN HERE
TO HIDE
YOU GOTTA LOVE THE PEOPLE FROM THE LOWER
EAST SIDE

SO WHO IS THE PRIDE OF THE LOWER EAST SIDE
THE PEOPLE ARE THE PRIDE OF THE LOWER EAST
SIDE
I SAID – WHO IS THE PRIDE OF THE LOWER EAST SIDE
THE PEOPLE ARE THE PRIDE OF THE LOWER EAST
SIDE

As all four of the guys stood there on that stage, looking out across the diversity of the audience, each one couldn't help but reflect back on memories of the past 50 years and what it took to make today a reality. People make up neighborhoods, and not realizing it, they develop their own stories. Here was a special story and it all began for four young guys on...*The Stoop!*

The Stoop – A Poem

GOLDEN DAYS
MAGIC NIGHTS
WE HANG OUT ON THE STOOP
CATCH ALL OF THE SIGHTS

A GATHERING PLACE
A PART OF OUR BEING
THE CENTER OF OUR UNIVERSE
FROM WHERE ALL COULD BE SEEN

A PEDESTAL, A PYRAMID
A MONUMENT IN STONE
A STAIRWAY TO THE STARS
WITH A HEART OF ITS OWN

A PLACE TO DREAM
OUR HEARTS DESIRES
TO ONE ANOTHER'S SOULS
WE FUEL THE FIRES

THE FIRES TO LIGHT
OUR WORLD TO COME
IT'S OUR TURN AT LIFE
IT'S OUR WALK IN THE SUN.

A STAGE TO PERFORM
OUR SWEET HARMONY
FROM THE SOUNDS OF OUR VOICE
COMES A STREET SYMPHONY

THE LIGHT FROM THE LAMP POST
AT THE END OF A DAY
BRINGS A SOFT BEAM OF WARMTH
ON THAT PLACE WHERE WE STAY

CLIMB THE STEPS OF OUR CASTLE
TO UNENDING FUN
FOR THE MANY WE WERE
WE ALL BECAME ONE, ON THE STOOP!

The Stoop – The Book

Ordering Information:

For individual copies of this book:

www.Amazon.com

Case-lot orders for resale, educational and non-profit purposes:

www.TheStoopMusical.com

The Stoop – The Musical

Production Information:

For information on licensing the script and music for theatrical purposes at educational institutions and non-profit community theatre venues:

www.TheStoopMusical.com

The Stoop – The Book

Ordering Information:

For individual copies of this book:

www.Amazon.com

Case-lot orders for resale, educational and non-profit purposes:

www.TheStoopMusical.com

The Stoop – The Musical

Production Information:

For information on licensing the script and music for theatrical purposes at educational institutions and non-profit community theatre venues:

www.TheStoopMusical.com